Caught Up:

The Beginning

DeJohnáy Harris

Love,
DeJohnáy
2021

To: Amiya Milan.

"You are my Sunshine, my lucky Sunshine."

Mommy loves you. You are my inspiration, and constant light to my world. I love you. You and God, are my reason, that I am here.

Acknowledgments

I never thought that this day would come. It has been a long journey, but I finally can say: "I'm officially an Author. "Writing has always been my first passion, and love. God gave me this gift, no matter how many times I stopped, and started. What really motivated me to continue writing, was a rough break up that I was going through. All the emotions I was going through, I decided to put it on paper.

It began with a short story challenge on Facebook. The feedback that I received from various people was amazing. So, I decided to make a group page, called "Caught Up: The Beginning (at the time). My storybook group gave me the push that I needed to finally complete my book.

I want to thank all the members, in my Facebook group. (Which is currently called, Lost Soul: short stories and more). They are my real true diehard fans. I also want to thank Jay Dunn. He is the artist, who designed the cover of my book. So, I just want to say: Thank You! To my friends, and family, thank you for supporting me.

I want to thank my mother, Delvetta Keyes. She is a leading example, as to always "Have Faith, and to trust, God" *"That he will never leave me, nor forsake me."*

This book has been, a long time coming. I am glad that this day has finally come. From the late-night posting, and miss spelled errors. From my computer crashing, and having to uploading the parts via my phone.

My readers loved, every bit of it. I'm just a Philly jawn, from Southwest. I've seen, and experienced some things. Some good and some bad, but through it all. I remain me. So, I hope you guys enjoy the story. Because this is just the beginning.

With Love,

DeJohnáy

Table of Contents

"As I woke up and let the sun kiss my face." "Rolling over looking at his beautiful face." "Wondering why this was happening again. I mean." "I promised myself this was the last time we would end up like this." "Fast forward to a "wyd." "Are you still up?" "Then my dumbass, giving into his smooth-talking ass." "As soon as my ass does that." "Boom! He coming over, at two in the morning." "And well you know the rest."

"See Jahmere is 6'3 caramel skin, tatted up body." "With a muscular built frame." "The sex, is amazing, and always on point." "Besides, I love this nigga." "It's just one little problem...

Chapter 1

Namira gets out the bed, rolling her eyes at Jahmere. As she heads into her bathroom, to shower. She

pugs in her curling irons, so she can start getting ready for work.

Jahmere is awaken, by the sound of the running water. He sits up in the bed, and rubs his eyes. Jahmere

gets out the bed, and checks his phone. He sees nobody has called him, and he heads into the bathroom.

He sees Namira in the shower, and he licks his lips. Jahmere, slowly opens the glass shower door.

Stepping in the shower, standing behind Namira.

"Good morning baby." Jahmere says, as he kisses on her neck. Turning Namira around, kissing on her

stomach. Putting one of her legs, on his shoulder.

Namira throws her head back, as she enjoys the pleasure. She can feel herself reaching a climax. As

Namira, is trying not to slip, in the shower. She can't help the moan, that is escaping from her mouth.

Jahmere sticks his tongue, inside of her pussy. Gently, sucking on her clit. Namira can feel, a tingling

sensation flow through her body. As she cums in Jahmere's mouth. She smiles, as she regains her

composure. Namira washes up. She is trying, to hurry up. So, she can ready for work. She gets out the

shower, and grabs her robe. Namira walks into her bedroom, grabbing her lotion off her vanity. She sits

down on the bed, and Jahmere comes out the shower. He comes walking, into the bedroom with a

towel, wrap around his body.

"See the problem with Jahmere." He has a wife and kids." "I know, you're probably thinking "bitch you the side bitch." "But it's not even like that." "Him and his wife or whatever, you want to call her." "They are separated for a while now."

"Plus, he says he is only there for their kids." "I know, it sounds like a bunch of bullshit." "But I believe him." "Then again, I get this feeling, that something isn't right."

Jahmere walks over to Namira, he kisses her on her forehead. Interrupting, her thoughts. Namira removes the towel, that is hiding his dick. She begins to caress it, until it is standing at attention. Jahmere lifts Namira up off the floor, and lays her on the bed. He spreads her legs, and enters her slow, and steady. Namira wraps her legs around his waist. As he thrust, deeper inside. Awaking a feeling, that is all too familiar. Namira pulls Jahmere closer to her body, kissing him on his neck.

"Shit." "Ya pussy wet." Jahmere whispers, under his breath. "Fuck." He says, thrusting into Namira deeper. He can feel the nut, rising in his dick. He picks up his tempo. As his cum leaves his dick, and enters into Namira. His breathing begins to slow down, and he kisses her on the lips. Jahmere goes back in the bathroom, and washes up again. He rushes to get dressed, so he can meet up with Bahshere. He grabs his keys, and tells Namira. He will call her later, as he is heading out the door. Jahmere stops in the doorway, and says. "What was it, that you wanted to talk about?"

Namira turns over on her stomach, and says "oh nothing." She says, waving Jahmere off. Not wanting to say, what is really on her mind. Jahmere kisses her again, and leaves. She stares, at the nightstand near her bed. Namira opens the drawer, and starring back at her, is a pregnancy test. From her OBGYN, confirming she is four weeks pregnant. *"Damn, how did I let this shit happen."*

Namira looks at her phone, she notices she has twenty minutes. She hurries, and gets ready for work. Namira grabs her keys, and bag. Rushing out her condo, and through the parking garage. Hopping in her Lexus coupe. Her iPhone begins to ring, it's Jahmere. She answers the phone, via Bluetooth.

"You at work, yet?" Jahmere asks. Making his way over, to the trap house. The one on, 18th and Diamond.

"Not yet." Namira says. "Since you wanted to make me late, and start this morning." She says, with a chuckle. Merging onto the exit, heading towards, downtown Philly.

"Naw you the one who dropped the towel." Jahmere responds, with a laugh.

"Well baby, let me get to work." Namira says, pulling into her parking spot. "I'm call you later." She says, before hanging up.

Namira gets out and rushes up to her office. In her six-inch, stilettos. The elevator doors open. Her secretary, Ashely greets her. "Good morning Ms. Wilson." She says, handing her a cup of green tea. "Your eight thirty appointment, is waiting for you." Namira looks down at her watch.

"Shit, its eight fort-five." She says to herself. Taking the cup from Ashely, and hurrying into her office.

"Sorry to keep you waiting." Namira says. Sitting the cup of tea, on her desk, and her purse under her seat. She pulls out, her client's wedding portfolio. So that they can, go over the last adjustments, for the wedding.

"So." Namira begins speaking, with a smile. "You said that, you want the color for the wedding to be-" She is interrupted, by her phone ringing. Namira excuses herself, and goes into her other office. She answers the phone, without looking at the caller id. "Baby I told you that I would call you."

"Baby." The female voice says, with an attitude. "Who dis?"

Namira rolls her eyes, because she already knows who it is. "You called my phone." She says, with an attitude.

"Yea bitch." The female voice says. "I'm trying figure out." "Why the fuck, ya name keep popping up, in my man phone." She continues to say, with an attitude.

"Listen *Va'Shay.*" Namira replies with a sigh. "You take that shit up with Jah." She says rolling her eyes. "I ain't got time to be arguing with you." Namira can't believe, she has the audacity to call her phone. "Matter fact, he was at my house last night." She says with sassiness. "With his head between my legs." Before Namira could even finish, letting Va'Shay have it. She hears Jahmere voice, in the background. "Yo give me my phone" he says, hanging up in Namira ear.

"I'm tired of this bullshit." Namira says to herself, trying to regain her composure. Namira relaxes her nerves, before she goes back out. She takes a deep breath, before she finishes up. Her meeting with her client.

That Evening

"He *playing in my face, on some nutshit."* Namira says to herself. Thinking about the phone call, she received from Va'Shay earlier. Namira has to tell Jahmere, about her being pregnant. It might go in the right direction. Then again, it might cause more drama. She is trying to enjoy her bath and relax, when her phone begins to ring. Namira looks at the caller id, she doesn't recognize the number. She answers it anyway, it could be her client calling. In regards to her wedding; which Namira doesn't need to lose. Or her fat check, that comes along with the wedding. So, she answers the phone call. "Hello."

"Yo, why the fuck, you block my calls!" Jahmere demands. His voice booming, through the phone. Namira forgot that she sent all Jahmere's calls to voicemail. She sucks her teeth, and lets out a sigh. "What do you want."

"I'm sorry about earlier." Jahmere says, in a softer tone.

"Whatever Jah, you full of shit." Namira says, hanging up her phone, and continues to enjoy her bath. A little while later, she gets out the tub. Grabbing her silk robe off the hook. Walking over to her vanity, so she can lotion up. She puts on a cute panty and bra set.

Admiring herself, in the full-length mirror. Namira touches her stomach, imagining how she is going to look. When her pregnancy begins to progress, further along. Namira thoughts are interrupted, by the locks being turned.

Jahmere comes into the condo, and the aroma of the food, hits his nose. "Damn baby, you cooked." He says, taking off his Timbs. Pushing them in the corner, by the door. Jahmere tosses his keys, on the table. He walks into her bedroom.

"Why the fuck, you keep playing Jah!" Namira yells, as she walks up to him. Not wasting no time, digging in his ass.

"What are you talking about?" Jahmere asks, grabbing around her waist. He really not trying to argue, and fight with her tonight. It's bad enough, Va'Shay always on some nutshit. Now Namira, wants to start her shit too. "Come on yo." "Not tonight."

"Why this bitch, calling my phone." Namira says. "Like, I thought ya'll wasn't together." She says, pushing, him away from her. Namira doesn't even want to argue. She walks into the kitchen, taking the chicken out the oven.

"Come on babe." Jahmere says. Following Namira into the kitchen. "I love you."

"Then why you ain't divorce her trifling ass, yet?" Namira says, turning to face Jahmere. "If you don't." Namira, begins to say. "Then me, and this baby are gone." She says, with her hand, on her stomach.

"The fuck you mean *baby*?" Jahmere asks. "You pregnant!" He says, with a confused look, on his face.

"You heard." "What the fuck *I*, just said." Namira says. Storming over to the nightstand, grabbing the papers, and pregnancy test. Namira enters back, into the living room. She throws the papers at him. "Yea, I knew what it was." She says. Throwing the papers at him. "I still continued, to mess around with you." Namira says in a way. As if, she should know better. "This shit has been going on, a year and half."

"Almost two years!" Namira says, raising her voice. "I want to know what are we doing?" She asks, wanting an honest answer from Jahmere. Namira figures, that regardless. Him and Va'Shay are still, legally married. Namira just looks at him, and rolls her eyes. "You know what." She says, with a scoff. "Don't say shit." Namira says, walking into her bedroom. Jahmere follows her, into the bedroom.

He walks over to Namira. "Back the fuck up." She says, pushing him out her personal space. "You kept, filling my head up with lies." Namira can't seem, to keep her emotions in order.

Jahmere walks up to Namira. "Can we please, go sit, and eat dinner." He says, pulling her closer to him. "Ya nigga hungry."

Namira rolls her eyes, and goes in the kitchen. She dishes up their food. Namira grabs the wine, from out the cabinet. Along, with two wine glasses. She then remembers, that she can't drink. "*Shit.*" Namira says to herself, as she sets the table. Jahmere comes into the dining room, and takes a seat. "So, what are you going to do." Namira says, with an attitude, and taking her seat at the table.

"What you mean?" Jahmere asks. "I'm take care, of my baby." He says. As if, that is an obvious answer.

"What about, you being married?" Namira asks. Putting a fork full of food, into her mouth.

"Man, come on with the bullshit." Jahmere says, with irritation in his voice.

"Every time I fucking mention, that you are still married." Namira says. "You get uptight." She says, pointing her fork at him.

"Listen, I'm trying to enjoy the night." Jahmere says. Not wanting, to arguing with her.

"Well then, get the fuck out!" Namira says, excusing herself from the table. She can feel the tears, forming in her eyes. Jahmere takes his time, getting up from the table. It seems that, all they do is; Fight, and argue about Va'Shay. He walks into the bedroom.

Jahmere wants to fully commit, to Namira. It's just him having to separate, himself from Va'Shay, completely. That not going to be an easy thing to do. She will make it her mission to make his life, miserable. When Va'Shay finds out, that Namira is pregnant. She will use this, as an excuse to fuck his life up.

About a half hour later, Jahmere comes out the shower. He dries off. He puts on a pair of, Calvin Klein boxers. He gets in the bed, and snuggles up against her. He puts his arms, around her. "Naw, get off of me Mere." Namira says dryly. Removing his arms, off her waist.

Jahmere sucks his teeth, and says. "Don't be like that." This is exact reason why, Namira is always complaining. Jahmere has this way, of making it seem. That everything, good between them.

"You treating this, like it's a fucking joke." Namira says, as tears fall, down her face.

"Baby don't cry." Jahmere says, wiping the tears, away. He kisses her lips, slowly making his way, to her neck. Namira can feel a warmth, beginning to form, between her legs. They look in each other eyes. As the moonlight dances, across their faces.

Namira just lays back, as Jahmere kisses lower. Reaching the top of her pussy, gently kissing on her clit. Which, sends an electric shock through her body. Jahmere sucks on her clit, with his juicy lips. Letting his tongue enter her, she lets out a soft moan. As her body begins, to levitate off the bed. Namira is gripping the sheets, she can feel the climax taking over her body. "Baby I'm about to cum!" Namira yelps out. Trying to run away from him, but he keeps her pinned down, on the bed. Jahmere inserts two fingers. Inside of her pussy, and simultaneously sucks on her clit.

"Ohh, my God baby!" "I'm cumin!" Namira moans, as she climaxes all his mouth. Jahmere just smiles.

He drinks, and slurps up her juices. As they flow, into his mouth. Jahmere comes back up, spreading

open her legs. Entering Namira with ease, and passion. She pulls him closer, to her body. "I Love you

Jah." She says looking into his eyes.

"Turn that ass around, for daddy." Jahmere says. As, Namira lay on her stomach, and arches her back.

He grabs her waist, speeding up his tempo. Namira looks back at Jahmere, as he thrust deeper into her.

Making her ass bounce, with each thrust. Namira matches, the tempo of his thrust. "Oh shit!" Jahmere

moans. "I'm about to bust!" Gripping her waist, even tighter. He can feel the nut, rising up his dick.

Making its way, to the head of his dick. "Ohh shiit!" Jahmere moans.

They both collapse, slowly in the bed. Laying in their sweat, and sex. Namira turns to Jahmere, and she

looks into his eyes. She takes a deep breath, and asks. "On some real shit." "Do you really, love me?"

"I love you yo." Jahmere says, as he kisses her lips. "Just rock out with me, a little bit longer."

Jahmere says. "Let me handle this." He says, looking Namira in her pretty, brown eyes.

Namira just smiles, part of her. Wants to believe Jahmere and what he is saying. Then the other apart of

her, has this weird feeling. That he isn't, being completely honest. She pushes the thoughts out her

mind. Namira doesn't want to go back and forth, with him. She just prays, that Jahmere, is telling her

the truth. Namira lays in his arms, and drifts off to sleep.

Chapter 2

The sun peaks through the window, and kisses her face. Namira is awakened, by a vibrating noise. She tries to go to sleep, but the vibration continues. Whoever keeps calling, won't stop. Jahmere is knocked out, snoring loudly. Namira gets out the bed. She picks up the phone, off the night stand. Namira looks at the caller id. It says *"Shay."* She answers the phone, with a sly smile. Speaking in the sweetest voice. "Hello."

"Who the fuck is this?" Va'Shay asks, with an attitude. "Where the hell is Jah!?" Va'Shay asks, with an attitude. "Bitchh give him the phone!" Va'Shay says. Basically, screaming through the phone.

"He is sleeping right now." Namira says, with sarcasm. "Can I take a message."

"When I see ya, hoe ass." Va'Shay says. Popping her gum, in Namira's ear. "I'm fuck you up."

Namira is really not for her, bullshit this morning. She ends the call, and sets his phone, back on the nightstand. Namira lays back down, to snuggle up under Jahmere. Later that morning, Namira is awakened. By a delicious smelling aroma, coming from the kitchen. She sits up, in the bed. Jahmere comes entering the bedroom, he has a tray full of food. Pancakes, sausages, eggs. Some home-fries, and some strawberries. With, a tall glass of orange juice. "Good morning baby." Jahmere says. Serving her breakfast, in bed. He places the tray in front of her. Feeding her, a fork full of eggs.

"Mmm, this is delicious." Namira says, kissing him on the lips.

"I gotta feed, both my babies." Jahmere says, kissing her stomach. "Babe look." "I have some business to handle." He says, getting up from the bed. Walking into the closet, so he can change his clothes.

"Damn already." Namira says, in a disappointing tone.

"I gotta go." Jahmere says, as he puts on his Balmain jeans, and fresh mint, colored Timbs. "I gotta get this fucking money." Reaching into his pocket, and pulling out, the rubber bands stacks. "Now that, you are carrying my baby." Tossing them, at the foot of the bed.

"Since when I needed you, to take care of me." Namira says, unimpressed by the cash.

"Come on, don't start." Jahmere says, pulling his Champion hoodie, over his head. "Look baby, I'm be by later." He says, shutting Namira up, with a kiss.

"Tell that bitch, stop calling." "Or, I'm whoop her ass!" Namira says, taking another bite of her food. Jahmere doesn't even respond, to what Namira just said. He doesn't need, another argument, this morning.

"Ard, I'm out." He says, grabbing his keys. Heading out the bedroom, and out the door.

Namira finishes her breakfast. She takes her shower and gets dress. Namira decides, she wants to go to the mall. So, she calls her bish Lee. "Wassup sis." "What you doing?"

"Nothing in the house." Leelee responds, dryly.

"You dressed?" Namira asks. "I wanna go to the mall."

"Where at?" Leelee asks, she figured. She could use, a little retail therapy.

"King of Prussia." Namira replies. Putting the dishes, in the dishwasher. "Jah drop some bread."

Leelee sucks her teeth, and rolls her eyes. "You still fucking with him."

"Sis, stop playing." Namira says laughing, starting the dishwasher. She walks in her bedroom, and grabs her Moschino purse. "Look I'm on my way." Namira says. "I got major tea for you bish." She says, before she hangs up. Namira grabs her keys, and heads out the door.

Twenty minutes later, she arrives at Leelee house. Leelee lives in the Roxborough/Manayunk area. She the definition of, badd and boujee. She can be ratchet as fuck, when needed. Leelee forevah a Philly chick, and don't mind letting motherfuckers know it either. "Hey bitchhh." Leelee says, getting into the car. Giving Namira a kiss, on the cheek. "Bish you slaying as usual." Namira says, complimenting Leelee on her outfit.

"Well you know." Leelee says, sticking out her tongue. "So, wassup, sis." She says, letting her Valentino bag, fall in her lap.

"Bihh!" Namira begins to say. "If I tell you the bullshit!" Namira says, pulling out Leelee's driveway, and heading towards the expressway.

"Bitch, I don't know why, you fuck with his ass." Leelee says, rolling her eyes.

"Cause his dick A1, and his pockets fat." Namira says, looking at Leelee.

Namira catches Leelee up, on the drama that has been going. As she gets off, at the exit. For the King of Prussia, mall. Namira enters into the parking lot, trying to find a spot to park in. She finds a parking spot, and she pulls in. They get out, and Leelee asks. "So, what you getting sis?" Putting her Valentino bag, over her shoulder.

"I wanna go into Lou first." Namira says, as they walk toward the entrance. "I want to see, if they have this bag I seen online." She says opening the door, as they walk inside of the mall. Leelee checks her phone, to see if she has any missed calls, from her nigga. Not one, notification. They head into, the Louis Vuitton store. The sales rep greets Namira, as she comes in. "Good morning Ms. Wilson." He says walking over, to give her a hug.

"Aye Tim, what you got for me?" Namira says, giving him a hug back.

"I just got these in this morning." Tim says, leading her into the private showroom. With Leelee following, right behind them. "This is the bag!" "I saw it online, last night." Namira says to Leelee. She picks up the bag, to get a better look. It's a leather bag, with light pink colored, calfskin details. With the LV lock and key, in Swarovski diamonds. "I'm take it." Namira says. "Can you put my initials, on the back of the lock?" She ask, handing the bag to the sales rep. "I'm going to pick it up later."

"Ohh of course Ms. Wilson." The sales rep replies. He then turns to Leelee. "What about you, Mrs. Peterson." Leelee looks around, she sees a brown, leather beauty case. It's shaped as a cylinder, and has the LV monogram. All over the bag. She picks it up, and says to the sales rep. "Did you guys get these ankle boots?" Leelee asks, as she describes the boots. "They are, a soft pink color." "The heel has the LV monogram, in the shape of a flower."

"I know which pair of shoes; you are talking about." Tim says, with excitement. "What size do you need?"

"Don't play with me Tim!" Leelee says, basically about to hyperventilate. "I need them in, a size seven."

"I'll be right back." Tim says, walking away. "Let me check the inventory." He says with a smile. "I believe we have your size." He says walking away, to get the shoes.

"He better not play with me today." Leelee says smiling. Pouring herself some champagne, having a seat.

Namira walks around, she gets a wallet, to match the hand bag. The sales rep comes back, with a smile on his face. He has the shoes in his hand. "You are in luck Mrs. Peterson." Tim says, walking up to Leelee. "This was the only pair, they sent." He says, walking up to Leelee. He couldn't give the shoes, to her fast enough. Leelee takes the box, setting the champagne flute on the table. She takes off her Valentino pumps. Namira tries on the boots. "What you think sis?" She asks Namira.

"Gurl, them shoes is fucking lit." Namira says. "I love them."

"I'll take them." Leelee says to the sales rep. Putting her Valentino pumps, back on. "I will be back later, to pick them up." Leelee says to the sales rep.

They leave and head into Saks and Bloomingdale's, for a couple more items. Then they stop in Victoria Secret and Namira tell Leelee the tea. Leelee rolls her eyes and says. "Speaking of the devil." Namira looks up and in walks. Jahmere's *soon to be, ex-wife* Va'Shay. Namira rolls her eyes turning her attention, back to picking out some more lingerie. Out the corner of her eye. Namira can see Va'Shay, coming towards her.

Va'Shay isn't ugly, but she not badd either. She just cute. Only thing she has, is a big ass. Which Va'Shay uses, to play these niggas. She is brown skin, standing at 5'8, and weighs a 180 pounds. You wouldn't be able to tell, because of her shape. She carries it in her hips, and ass.

"Didn't I tell you." Va'Shay says, stepping in Namira's face. "Next time I see you, that I'm whoop ya ass!"

"Hold up bitch." Leelee says, walking up on Va'Shay. "I know, you not stepping to sis." She says, standing next to Namira. Va'Shay ignores Leelee completely. She turns to Namira, and says. "I told you to leave Jah alone."

Namira steps in Va'Shay face. "Bitch, I ain't gotta do shit." Namira says, stepping in Va'Shay face.

"But keep fucking him." She says with a smirk. "You need to be checking him."

"But I'm telling you this shit to ya face." Namira says. "I'm not going to stop fucking, sucking, or being with him." She says looking Va'Shay up and down. "He doesn't want to be with you. "If he did, he wouldn't be chasing around me all the time." "Matter of fact, from what he tells me." "Jah just there for ya'll kids, and that's it Va'Shay."

That's when Va'Shay flips, her long 36-inch, Malaysian weave. She points her finger, in Namira face. "You got one more time, to run ya mouth."

"So, what you trying to do bitch." Namira says, squaring up. Preparing to whoop Va'Shay ass, in the store.

Va'Shay tries to hit Namira, but Leelee is already on her ass. Punching her all in, her face and head. "I told you bitch, stop playing with my sis." Leelee says. As she is whooping Va'Shay ass. Namira is trying to break the fight up. It is starting to get, out of control. They don't need, to get locked up in Montgomery County. They will lock all three of them up, without no hesitations.

"See my bitch, originally from Strawberry Mansion projects." "So, she with, the shits."

Namira manages to break the fight up, before security comes. They leave the items, that they were going to buy. "That bitch, really get on my fucking nerves." Leelee says, walking into the restroom. She checks her face and hair. Making sure she doesn't have any marks.

"Lee." Namira says. "Let's go get our stuff." Namira says. She still in shock, Va'Shay would even try the bullshit. They walk back to her car, and Namira puts her bags in the trunk. "Bitch can you believe her." Namira says, as they get back in the car.

"I told you Jah, got his drama." Leelee says, rolling her eyes. "So, I'm ride with you, through whatever."

"I'm hungry, let's do Maggiano's." Namira says, pulling into the parking lot. "I know, I just." Namira begins to say. "Come on, I'm hungry." She says, switching the subject, and heading inside.

They wait, as the hostess finds them a table. The hostess, tells her to follow her, to their table. Namira sits down, and the hostess, gives them their menus. "Can we start with some cocktails." Leelee says wasting no time. "I want a Margarita." She says, looking at the menu. "Bitch what you getting?" Leelee says turning to Namira, as the waiter comes up.

"Good, afternoon, ladies." "My name is Jasper, your waiter." He says with a smile. "What would you like?"

"Can I get a club soda, with lemon." Namira says smiling.

"Bitch, what." Leelee says. "Naw, she going to have."

"A club soda, with lemon please." Namira says, finishing Leelee sentence. The waiter, continues to take their orders. Namira orders, a salad with baked salmon. Leelee orders, the chicken alfredo. Jasper leaves from the table. So, he can, put their orders in.

"Bitch, you better not be pregnant." Leelee says, giving Namira the side eye.

"Well." Namira says. Rubbing her stomach and smiling.

"Bitch, no!" Leelee says, getting excited. "Does Jah know?" She says in a whispering tone.

"Yea, I told him." Namira says, rolling her eyes. "He still *married,* to this bottom bitch hoe."

"Mira, I told ya ass." Leelee says, taking a sip of her margarita.

"I know sis." Namira says softly. "I knew what the fuck it was." She says, letting out a sigh. "Now, we about to have a baby."

"I will cap his ass." Leelee says. "If he doesn't get it together." Namira can't help but laugh. Deep down, she knows that Leelee is serious. "Sis, relax please." She says laughing.

"I just have to let it, be known." Leelee says. "I don't play when it comes to you sis." She says, taking another drink, of her margarita. They enjoy their food, and continue to catch up.

Chapter 3

Shortly after, Namira drives Leelee back home. They exchange their goodbyes. Leelee tells Namira, to call her when she gets home. Namira promises that she will, as she pulls off. Namira gets on the expressway, heading back to her condo. As she is driving. Namira is getting an incoming call, from Jahmere. She doesn't answer, because she is five minutes, away from home. Jahmere texted, her earlier. Asking if, they could go out for dinner. So that, must be why he is calling her. Namira pulls into the parking garage, and parks her Lexus coupe. She gets out the car, grabbing her purse. Namira gets the shopping bags, out the trunk. She is walking through the parking garage. Heading up, to her condo. Namira grabs her keys, out her Dior purse. Just when she was about to turn the lock, Jahmere opens the door. "Aww thanks baby." She says walking in, placing the bags by the door.

Jahmere doesn't say anything. He goes back over to the couch, and finishes rolling his L. Namira slips out her Prada pumps, and puts her Dior shades on the table. She walks over to him, sitting on the couch blowing a L. "Hey baby." Namira says. Trying to kiss him on the lips, but Jahmere moves his face.

"Why the fuck." Jahmere says. "I hear about you, Shay, and Lee, getting into a fight today." He says blowing smoke. In her direction, giving her the death stare. *"No, this bitch didn't run and tell him."* *"Like this nigga going do something, or check me"* Namira says to herself.

"I didn't start with that bitch." Namira says, sucking her teeth. "She called herself getting tough, and she got beat the fuck up." "The end."

"If anything, you should be asking me am I okay." Namira says with irritation. "Being as though, I'm carrying ya fucking baby." She says, getting up. Walking into the kitchen, so she can get a glass of water.

"What the fuck did I say to you!" Jahmere says, following behind Namira. "It ain't easy!" "I got fucking kids" he says yelling.

"*I'm* about to have *your baby*!" Namira says, getting in his face.

"You foul, you know that." Jahmere says, as he walks away. He puts out the L, and tucks it behind his ear. Jahmere grabs his keys and phone. He starts walking towards the door. Namira follows after him, and blocks the door, so he can't leave.

"No pussy you the foul one." Namira says, moving from the door, so he can leave. "Give me fucking keys too!" She says, with anger. They never argued like this. Namira is starting to feel. Jahmere should understand, the position that she is in. For him to flip the situation. Making it seem like, it's her fault.

"I'm out." Jahmere says, throwing the keys on the floor. Namira slams the door, and she slides down on to the floor. The tears are rolling down her face. She is tired of the bullshit with Jahmere. Then on top of it all, she finds out she is pregnant. Like, this should be a happy time for them both. Yet, Jahmere is thinking that, how she feels. It doesn't matter.

Namira goes into her bedroom, and goes into her private bathroom. She opens the medicine cabinet, and grabs the bottle of Tylenol. Namira goes into the dining room, and gets her phone out her purse. She walks back in her bedroom, and dials Jahmere number. Waiting for him to answer, after the third ring, he answers. "Jah, come home please." She says between tears. Sitting on the bed, with the bottle of pills, still in her hand.

"I told you to rock with me." Jahmere says. "I need some space right now." He says, letting out a sigh.

"You need some space?!" Namira says with an angry tone. "I'm pregnant." She says with a scoff. "Now, you need space." "How the fuck, does that work!" Namira says, yelling.

"You knew what the situation was." Jahmere says, out of frustration. "You made the decision, to keep fucking with me."

"Yea." Namira says, with sarcasm. "You made it seem, ya'll wasn't together!" "So, ya'll fucking, is that it?" Namira asks, really wanting to know. Va'Shay comes walking, into the living room. Being extra, she was listening to the whole conversation. Va'Shay decides, this is the perfect time to be petty. *"Jah, baby come on the kids need you to."* Va'Shay says. Faking the sweetest voice, being loud enough. So that Namira can hear her, through the phone.

"You know what it's cool." Namira says, with a calmness. "Consider me, and you the fuck over." She says, hanging up in his ear. Namira still has the bottle of Tylenol, in her hand. *"How can he just not want me, or our baby?"* She says to herself. Namira untwists the top, and pours them into her mouth. A tear runs down her cheek, she wipes it away. As she goes into the kitchen, and grabs the bottle of Blair, out of the refrigerator.

At this point, Namira isn't thinking about the baby. That is forming into her stomach. She untwists the top, and takes the bottle, and guzzles the liquor down, as she begins to walk back to her room. Namira makes it to her bedroom door, and slides down to the floor. Laying on the plush carpet. Letting the effects of the pills and alcohol runs its course. Her body begins to shake violently. Namira iPhone begins to ring, as her eyes begin to close…

Meanwhile in Overbrook

"Why the fuck you keep playing Jah." Va'Shay says. "I'm not going the fuck nowhere" She says, folding her arms.

"Why you keep thinking, we still together." Jahmere says. "I told ya dumb ass, we over." He says, ready to fuck Va'Shay up.

"Since when!" Va'Shay says, raising her voice. Jahmere grabs Va'Shay, by her throat. "Don't think, I forgot, bout you and Bah." He says, squeezing he throat. "Only reason ya ass still breathing, is because you got my kids." Va'Shay is trying to get his hands, from around her neck. She can't because of Jahmere's grip. "L-l-let me go, Jah." She manages, to utter.

"We been over!" Jahmere says, he can feel his anger raising. "Your gold-digging ass, ain't shit!" He says. Loosening his grip, from round her neck.

When Jahmere found out Va'Shay, fucked Bahshere. He called it quits. He moved out their home, that he bought. Jahmere decided, that he would strictly be around for his kids, only. Jahmere made sure Va'Shay was well, taken care of. As far as their marriage was concerned, it was over. When it comes to him, and Bahshere. It's just strictly business. He doesn't look at him, as his right handz, anymore.

It's nothing, she can say. Everything she has, is because of Jahmere. Va'Shay thought, having his kids. That would be her golden ticket, into having Jahmere's money, at her fingertips. It just not as easy, as she thought it would be. So now she has to come up with a new plan. Her lifestyle is expensive, and she be damned if she has to give it all up.

"Baby." Va'Shay says. Trying to think, of a way. That she can continue, to be on Jahmere's good side. Jahmere phone, begins to ring. He looks at the caller id, and its Leelee. "Yo sis."

At Namira's Condo

Leelee is calling Namira phone, nonstop. She hasn't been responding to her texts, or calls. Something doesn't seem right, to Leelee. She decides to go over, and check on Namira. She hops, in her Mercedes C-class. Leelee pulls into the parking garage, barely parking her car in the spot. She heads up to Namira's condo, and she knocks on the door. "Namira!" Leelee calls out, but still no answer. She goes in her purse, and gets the spare key.

Leelee turns the locks, and goes inside. She puts her purse and keys, on the table. Leelee walks toward, the bedroom. She can feel this weird feeling, forming in her stomach. As she walks in Namira's bedroom. "Oh my God!" Leelee says, rushing over to her. "Mira!" She says, checking her pulse. Leelee grabs her phone, and dials 911. She explains to the operator, what happened. Leelee gives, the operator the address, to Namira's condo. The operator advises Leelee, to perform CPR. Until the paramedics arrive, and she hangs up. She calls Jahmere. "Jah you have to come quick its Namira." "She's not breathing!" She says in a panicking tone. "I think she tried to kill herself." Leelee says, still giving her CPR.

"What!" Jahmere yells. As his voice, booms through the phone. "I'm on my, fucking way!" He says, hanging up.

"Baby girl, please don't leave me." Leelee says, crying. "Why would you do this, why!" She manages to get a pulse. The paramedics arrived shortly, with the stretcher and the gurney. "I managed to get a pulse." Leelee says, as the paramedics take over. "She still, is unconscious."

"Okay, Ma'am." One of the paramedics says, to Leelee. "Step aside, we got it from here." The other paramedic, puts an IV in her arm. They load Namira on the gurney, and wheel Namira down and out, of her condo. Leelee is right behind them. Grabbing her purse, and keys. They load Namira, into the back of the ambulance. "We have to get her, to the hospital now!" The paramedic says, to Leelee.

"Which one are you taking her to?" Leelee asks, trying to remain calm.

"University of Penn." The paramedic says, before they pull off.

Jahmere, and Bahshere show up. He barely parks the car, before they get out. "Aye yo sis!" Jahmere says. Getting out the car, and walking towards her. "What the fuck happened sis?!"

Leelee slaps Jahmere. "Nigga all this shit, is because of you!" She says, because she knows. That it is because of Jahmere, that she tried to kill herself.

Bahshere grabs Leelee. "Aye yo, baby, chill out." He says, before Leelee, really fuck Jahmere up.

"Don't tell me to chill out." Leelee says, pointing her finger at Bahshere. She knew something like this, would happen. Ever since her brother passed, Namira hasn't been the same.

"I swear to God, if she doesn't fucking make it." Leelee says to Jahmere. "I'm put a fucking bullet, right between ya eyes." She says, walking off. Getting into her Mercedes C-class, and speeding toward the hospital. "God please let her be okay." Leelee says. "I can't take this." She says. Looking up to the night sky, and speeding through the red lights. Leelee quickly pulls up, to the entrance of the hospital, handing her keys to the valet. Rushing into the emergency room. "Hi, I'm here to see, Namira Wilson." Leelee says to the receptionist.

The receptionist, types in here name. "Yes, can you have a seat." She says, picking up the phone. "I'm page the doctor." Leelee iPhone rings. She sucks her teeth, when she realizes who it is. "Hello." She answers with irritation. "They got me waiting here now, she's at University."

Bahshere and Jahmere arrive, ten minutes later. Jahmere walks up to Leelee. "What are they saying?" He asks, worried about Namira.

"Nigga, don't act like you fucking care, now." Leelee says angrily.

The doctor comes out, to the waiting area. He calls out *"Wilson."* They all, walk up to the doctor. "Is she okay?" Leelee says. "Can we see her now?"

"Everybody, just calm down." The doctor says, putting up his hands. Signaling for them, to calm down.

"What about the baby?" Leelee asks, in a worried tone.

The doctor lets a sigh, before speaking. "Because Ms. Wilson, overdosed." "As well as, mixing the alcohol." "One of the fetuses, didn't make it-"

"Wait, wait a minute." Jahmere says. "You saying, she was carrying twins?" He asks, waiting for confirmation.

"Yes." He says, opening up her chart. "She is a little, over five weeks." The doctor says, putting their minds at ease. "The ultrasound shows, no abnormalities." He says, looking over the notes. "Follow me, so you guys can see her." The doctors say, walking them to the elevators. "She is sedated." The doctor says, as they get on the elevator.

"We had to sedate her, because of the reaction." The doctor says, walking them to her room. "From the alcohol, and the pills." He opens the door, so that they could go inside. Leelee is the first one, to enter into her room. She walks up to Namira's bed. "Hey sis." Leelee says, grabbing her hand. Jahmere walks over slowly. Seeing her like this, is something he is not used too. "Baby, I'm so fucking sorry." Leelee rolls her eyes. She knows that Jahmere, is the cause of the bullshit.

Bahshere notices the tension, between Leelee and Jahmere. He walks over to her, and says. "Aye yo bae." He says, gently putting his hands, on Leelee shoulder. "Let them, have some alone time." Noticing how quiet Jahmere is, and this is a difficult time. Seeing Namira, in the predicament, that she is in.

"Fuck him!" Leelee says, raising her voice. "He the reason she like this, in the first place!" She says. Not hiding her anger towards Jahmere.

"Let's go get something, out the café." Bahshere says, leading Leelee out the room. He doesn't need another fight, between her and Jahmere. Especially, at this time.

"I swear I didn't mean for this shit to happen." Jahmere says, holding her hand. "It just a lot of shit going on." Namira eyes begin to open, as Jahmere is holding her hand. Jahmere can feel Namira's hand moving. He looks up, and her eyes are open. The expression on her face, says it all.

"Why are you the fuck here?!" Namira says, not wanting him in her presence. Jahmere feels really bad, seeing Namira in this condition. "Baby, lay down you need to rest." Jahmere says, not wanting to upset her. Or, even the baby for that matter.

Leelee, and Bahshere are coming back from the cafeteria, when Leelee notices. Jahmere, and Namira talking. "What happen?" Leelee says rushing, over to Namira's side.

"Aye bro let's go." Bahshere says, to Jahmere. Letting Leelee, and Namira have their privacy.

"I lost one of my babies Lee." Namira says crying, in Leelee's arms. Leelee doesn't say anything, she just holds Namira hand, tightly. "Why would you do this? She asks, looking Namira in her eyes.

"Me, and Jah got into it." Namira says, with an attitude. "He found out, about the fight." "Between us, and Shay." She says, sitting up in the bed. "So, then he starts calling me foul." Namira says. "It got heated, so I told him give me keys, and leave."

"That's why, she got her ass beat." Leelee says, referring to Va'Shay.

"Wait, so we arguing." Namira says, continuing with the conversation. "He called me foul." "Saying that, because he has kids with her." "Just all this bullshit." Namira says, rolling her eyes.

"What the fuck!" "That gotta do with ya'll." Leelee says. "Ain't *you* bout to have his baby." She asks. Not believing, how Jahmere is acting.

"Exactly." Namira says, as the tears, roll down her face. "So, I call his phone." She says. "His dumbass, was over her crib."

"Who Shay's?!" Leelee says, getting upset.

"Yea." Namira says, wiping the tears away. "That bitch was talking shit, through the phone."

"Fuck that bitch!" Leelee says, with venom. "I'm fuck Jahmere up!" "He supposed, to be ya nigga." She says, feeling the anger boiling inside of her. "Yet, he still entertaining that fucking smut."

"Sis, please just calm down." Namira says, in a groggy tone. "I'm getting tired." She says, with a sleepy tone. "Just sit with me." Namira says, patting the side of the bed.

Leelee says a quick prayer, as she sits on the bed. She can't help but feel, that somehow this is her fault. If she didn't introduce, Jahmere to Namira. Then none, of this shit would be happening.

"When I found out, that they were fucking." "I decided, to teach her whore ass a lesson." "That's all that bitch is good for." "So, I played match maker, between Jah and Mira." "Jahmere was over Shay, so I thought this was the perfect idea." "I know you probably thinking: "Why the fuck, you stay with Bahshere lying ass as for then." "I don't know, I guess you can say it's love." "Damn that don't make me no better huh." Leelee is so consumed, by her own thoughts. She didn't even hear; the doctor enters into the room.

"Hi, Mrs. Peterson." He says, to Leelee. "My name is Dr Thompson." "Can I talk to you, about Namira's health?"

"Yea sure." Leelee says, letting out a sigh. Looking over her shoulder at Namira, as she sleeps soundly.

"In my best interest." Dr Thompson says. "That Ms. Wilson be kept, for a Psychological evaluation." He says, waiting for Leelee to respond. " I would need you to sign off." He says getting out a pen. "On her paperwork, on her behalf."

"Where do I sign." Leelee says, to Dr Thompson. As he opens the folder, and pulls out the paperwork. Leelee doesn't want Namira, to keep going off the deep end. She just prays that Namira, never finds out. How Say'Von was murdered, cause if she does, it would just crush her.

The Next Morning

Namira slowly opens her eyes. Her room is surrounded, with bouquet of flowers. It was so many flowers; you would think she was dying. The nurse comes into the room, and smiles at Namira. "Ms. Wilson you're up."

"What happened." Namira says, trying to get her thoughts together. "Who are all these flowers from?"

"I'm not sure." The nurse says. Taking Namira's vitals, and changing her IV bag. "Whoever sent them." "Must really love you." The nurse gets one of the cards. "It's signed Jah?"

"How is my baby." Namira says, with worry in her voice. Putting her hand, on her stomach. The nurse reassures her, that everything is fine. Jahmere comes, walking in the room. You could cut the tension, with a knife. Namira cuts her eyes at him. "What are you doing here?"

"I'm going to give you guys, some privacy." The nurse says, leaving the room.

"Baby, you like the flowers." Jahmere says, walking over to Namira. Trying to give her a kiss, but she turns her face away.

"Why the fuck is you here?" Namira asks, with disgust in her voice.

"I'm sorry Mira." Jahmere says, lowering his head. "Listen, I was being a fucking dickhead." "Shit, just complicated-"

"The fuck you mean *"it's complicated."* Namira says, mocking Jahmere. "Nigga get a divorce." "That simple!" She says, raising her voice. Namira is tired of the indecisiveness. Its either; He wants to be with her, and *their* baby. As well, as still being able. To take care of his other kids. Or, loose Namira, and the baby altogether. "Let me ask you this." Namira says, folding her arms. "Are you legally separated?"

"Yes, but its more to it, than that." Jahmere says, trying to explain.

"So, explain nigga." Namira says with an attitude. "Because *"we"* are about to have, *our own baby*." She says. "Your other kids aren't the problem." Namira says, rolling her eyes. "It's that *bitch* Shay." Jahmere knows Va'Shay will make it difficult. Especially, when it comes to him. Spending time with his kids. Va'Shay will go as far, as getting him busting. Just out of spite. "Baby please." He says, taking a deep breath. "I need you, to be my rock." He says, gently grabbing onto her chin. Looking into her beautiful eyes. Namira can't deny her feelings. She loves Jahmere, and want to make their relationship work. It's just difficult, when he has a baby mom, who is crazy. "Baby don't cry." Jahmere says, wiping the tear away.

Dr Thompson comes in, breaking up the moment. "Hey, Ms. Wilson how are you feeling?"

"Better." Namira says, sitting up in the hospital bed. She just really want to go home.

"That's good." Dr Thompson says, opening up his chart. "Your being transported, to our psych ward."

"Wait what!" Namira says, interrupting him. "Why I'm fine."

"We think, it would be in your best interest." Dr Thompson begins to say, but Namira interrupts him.

"Who the fuck is *we.*" Namira says, getting an attitude.

"Mrs. Peterson." Dr Thompson says. "We spoke, last night." "She has already signed off, on your paper work." Namira lets out this big sigh. Knowing Leelee wouldn't do this, if wasn't serious. "If everything goes well." Dr Thompson says. "You will be able to leave, within seventy-two hours." He says, trying to give her, some type of optimism.

"Am I allowed to go with her." Jahmere asks, the doctor.

"I'm sorry sir, we haven't meet." Dr Thompson says, extending his hand.

"I'm her boyfriend." Jahmere replies, shaking the doctor's hand.

"I'm sorry." Dr Thompson says. With a little bit, of sadness in his voice. "For the first, twenty-four hours." "There are no visitors." He says, with a bit of disappointment.

Jahmere notices the scared look, on Namira face. "Baby listen." He says. "I'll come see you, when I can." Kissing Namira, on the lips. Dr Thompson leaves. The nurse come in, with the wheelchair.

Rolling it, to the edge of the bed. Jahmere helps Namira, into the wheelchair. "You know, I Love you right." He says, looking into her beautiful eyes.

"Okay we have to go." The nurse says. Trying to rush, Namira out her room.

"Ard, hold up." Jahmere says, with an attitude. "It's something, I need to say." He gently grabs, both Namira's hands. "I know." Jahmere says. Looking her, directly in her eyes. "I haven't been the best nigga." He says, letting out a sigh. "I put you through, a lot of bullshit."

"I love you, Mira." Jahmere says, bending down on one knee. Taking Namira left hand, pulling out a little blue, Tiffany and Co box.

"Umm Jah." Namira says, with excitement. "Is this, what I think it is!" She says, smiling.

Jahmere opens up, the box. "Will, you marry me?" He asks. Inside the box, is a seven-caret. White gold, princess cut diamond ring.

"Yes baby!" Namira says. Holding her hand, over her mouth. "Yes, I will marry you." She says crying, and hugging him tightly.

"Babe, I can't breathe." Jahmere says, chuckling. "Let me put it on your finger first." He says chuckling, placing the ring on her finger.

"I love it." Namira says, admiring the ring. "And, I Love you." She says, hugging Jahmere tightly.

"Okay Ms. Wilson." The nurse says. "We really have to go." Bringing, the happy moment to an end.

Jahmere watches, as they go down the hall, disappearing out of his sight. That's when his phone starts

to ring. He looks down at the caller id and its Bahshere. "Yo." Jahmere answers.

"Aye yo, where you at nigga?" Bahshere asks, not wasting no time.

"I'm leaving the hospital now." Jahmere says, leaving out the room. "I was visiting Mira." He says,

heading out to the hospital exit. "Wassup?"

"Meet me at the trap spot." Bahshere says. "The one up Cambria." He says, putting out the black and

mild. Not wanting to discuss anything else, over the phone.

"Ard, I'm on my way." Jahmere says, hanging up the phone. Walking through the parking lot. It's

killing him to see her like this. His trap spot in Cambria, makes the most money. Jahmere doesn't need

another thing to be fucking up. He hops in his Benz, and speeds through the parking lot, so he can meet

up with Bahshere.

Chapter 4

Penn Medicine Behavioral Health and Mental Services

"Good Morning Ms. Wilson." She says, with a smile. "My name is Dr. Benson." "I will be your therapist, for the next seventy-two hours." She says with a smile. "Do you know why you are here?" Dr Benson asks, trying to break the tension.

"Yea." Namira says dryly. "I tried to kill myself." She replies, with aggravation.

"Can you tell me." Dr Benson asks. "Why, you wanted to hurt yourself?" She says, wanting to start the session. With simple questions.

"I'm good." Namira replies, with a short answer. "I'm sitting here, talking to a fucking shrink." She says, chuckling, to herself.

"I'm sensing, some hostility." Dr Benson responds, calmly. Not being bothered, by Namira's rudeness.

"Yes, I don't fucking, wanna be here." Namira says, with frustration. "I'm missing out on my shmoney." She says crossing her arms. "I need to go home, so I can be with my man."

"You'll able to do that." Dr Benson says, in a calm tone. "The hospital takes, these types of incident serious." "Especially, when you are carrying a child." She says. With seriousness, in her voice.

Namira doesn't feel comfortable, opening up to her feelings. It's too much pain, that still remains. She just doesn't want to re-live, or re-visit the memories. "What are you feeling, right now?" Dr Benson asks. Noticing the body language, that Namira is presenting. Namira continues, to ignore Dr Benson. Her mind drifts back, to that dreadful day…

December 21, 2016

"Mira." Leelee says, with sadness in her voice. She trying to get the words out, but her mouth won't let her speak.

"Lee what's wrong?" Namira asks, noticing the sadness in her voice. "What happened?"

Leelee is quiet. She can't seem, to get the words out. "Y-y-you gotta come quick!" Leelee says, stammering. "It's your brother."

Namira's heart, begins to sink. She can feel, this churning forming, in her stomach. "Where are you?"

"I'm at the city morgue." Leelee say, crying. "J-just come quick." Namira hangs up the phone. She screams at the top of her lungs. She can't believe, what she just heard. Namira grabs her keys, and puts on her Ugg boots. She is speeding, toward the morgue. Trying not to slip, on the snow and salt, covered road.

Philadelphia City Morgue

Leelee hands are shaking. She replays, that conversation in her head: "Sis, you gotta help me."

Va'Shay says, with desperation.

"Why you ain't meet up, for the drop!" Leelee says, basically yelling through the phone.

"It's Say'Von." "I- I-I set him up." Va'Shay says finally. Trying to act, as if she is remorseful.

"You did what!" Leelee says. "Bitch are you stupid!" She says, getting up, from the couch. "Where

you at?" Leelee says, putting on some clothes, and grabbing her keys.

"I'm at his crib now." Va'Shay says, pacing the floor. "Can you come get me?"

"Stay right there." Leelee says. I'm on my way." She says, before hanging up. Leelee is not sure, what

type of bullshit Va'Shay pulling. But she is about to find out. She throws on her leather jacket, and her

combat boots. Rushing out her house, and towards her car. She speeds off, not aware of the conditions,

of the roads. Leelee is calling Va'Shay phone, but it's going to voicemail. She gets to the house, and

parks her Lexus. She grabs her 9mm mag out the glove compartment, and hops out the car.

The front door is wide open. Leelee heads up the steps, and enters the house, with caution. She

pulls out her 9mm, calling out Va'Shay name. Still no answer. Leelee hears, somebody crying out; for

help. She follows the cry, and on the floor, is Say'Von. "Ohh my God!" Leelee says, rushes over to him.

She can see, he is bleeding, out the side of his stomach. Leelee dials 911, and trying to stop the blood, at the same time. *"Bro I'm sorry." "Yes, I need an ambulance, to 223 Dauphin Street please."* Leelee

says, before she hangs up. She keeps applying pressure, to Say'Von wound.

"Make sure, you take care of my sister." Say'Von says slowly. Trying not to choke, on his blood. That

is starting, to fill his lungs. *"Look after Namira for me, and tell her I Love her."* Say'Von says, as his

breathing begins to slow down.

"You are going to be okay." Leelee says, trying to comfort Say'Von. *"Everything is going to be fine,*

just breath slowly." She watches, as Say'Von eyes slowly close. His breathing stops. Leelee can't stop

the tears, from falling. She just sits there, till the paramedics come.

Everything seems to be, moving in slow motion. The cops arrive, and take her statement. Leelee

lies about, what has happened. She makes up a story, saying she was driving pass. That Leelee heard

some gunshots, and somebody was running out his house. When the cops questioned Leelee, asking if

she seen anybody. She responds, with a no. They asked her, how does she know the victim. Leelee

explains that she doesn't know him. Leelee can't let anything, get back to her. Or Jah, or even

Va'Shay. After the cops take, Leelee statement. She goes home, to change her clothes. That's when she

calls Namira. Telling her, to meet her at the city morgue. It seems, everything that Va'Shay touches; it

seems to go bad.

Namira rushes into the morgue. She sees Leelee, sitting down. "What happened!" She says, rushing over to her. "Lee!" "What the fuck, happened?!" Namira says, with tears down her eyes.

Leelee, can't seem to tell Namira, the truth. The look on her face, says it all. "He's gone Namira." She says, between tears. "I-" "A neighbor, found him." Leelee says, lying. "He was in the house, not breathing." "So, they called the cops."

"Why would somebody do this, to me." Namira says, crying in Leelee arms. "Why!" "He was all, that I had left." She feels that her heart, has been ripped out of her chest. Namira can't seem to breathe, as she breaks away from Leelee. All Namira can do is cry, the tears stream down her face.

"So, Ms. Wilson." Dr Benson says. Breaking Namira, out of her trance. "Let's talk about your childhood." The tears continue, to fall down Namira's face. She doesn't want to talk, about her past. It's too painful. "Let's try this tomorrow." Dr Benson suggest. She can see, something, is bothering her.

Namira takes a deep breath, before she speaks. "My mother, and father were killed, in front of me." "I was eight years old, when it happened." She takes a deep breath, before continuing. "Then two years ago, my brother was murdered." Namira finally says.

Dr Benson gets up. "We can finish this session, tomorrow." She says, grabbing some Kleenex tissues, off her desk. Handing the tissues to her. Dr Benson, doesn't want to push the issue, any further.

"I want the help." Namira says. Trying to keep her cool, and open up. Namira begins to tell the story,

of how her parents died. Going, into detail, of her brother being murdered. Namira talks about, her

relationship with Jahmere. What happened, and what led her to this point; of her trying to kill herself.

"Can I ask you something, Ms. Wilson?" Dr Benson says, with caution. "This Leelee, your best

friend." "How long, have you known her?" She says, referring to her previous notes.

"We've been best friends." "Since our last year, of high school." Namira says, not liking the way. This

conversation is going. "Why are you asking me about her?"

Dr. Benson takes a deep breath, before answering. "On two separate occasions, you mention Leelee."

"I never had, to question her loyalty." Namira says, interrupting her.

"Okay." Dr Benson says, shrugging her shoulders. "Maybe you need, to re-evaluate your friendship."

"Can we stop." Namira says, getting pissed off. "I'm getting tired." She says, with sarcasm.

"Sure Ms. Wilson." Dr Benson says, closing her notebook.

Namira leaves the office, and goes to call Jahmere. "Hey baby." She says, as soon as Jahmere answers.

"I miss you."

"I miss you too." Jahmere says. "Naw!" "I need that fucking shipment tonight!" He says, yelling through the phone. "Baby, I'm handling some business." Jahmere says. Shifting his focus, back on Namira. "I'm be up there, tomorrow."

"Okay, I love you." Namira says, hanging up the phone. She walks back to her room, and she sits on the bed. Namira lets out this sigh. Namira lays down in the bed, rubbing her stomach. She feels awful, for what she did. It's seems, the more her and Jahmere fight. The more, he is pulling away from her. Despite, how their relationship started; Its now on the line. Namira, just closes her eyes, and drifts to sleep.

Later that Night…22nd and Cambria

Bahshere pulls out his silencer. The red dot, dances over his forehead. "Come on man please!" He says, begging for them not to kill him. "You can ask Bah, he was the one who-" Before he could utter, another word. Bahshere shots him, with the silencer. In the forehead. "Well now, ya dead ass know." Jahmere says, with no remorse. Watching his body, slump on the floor. The floor begins to soak, with his blood. Jahmere leaves out the trap house.

All he can think about, is Namira. His thoughts are interrupted, by his phone ringing. Jahmere looks down, and "*Shay.*" Flashes, across the screen, as Jahmere answers the call. "He's dead!" Va'Shay says, crying. "My brother Ricky!" Jahmere hangs up the phone, because this is just beginning. He feels that, Va'Shay has to pay, and starting with her brother. This is just the beginning….

48 Hours Later

"So, Ms. Wilson how." Dr Benson says. Trying to start off, the conversation. "How are you doing, this

morning?" "Can you cut the bullshit." Namira says. Getting straight, to the point. "Am I able, to go

home tomorrow." She asks, folding her arms.

"That all depends, on today's session." Dr Benson says, with sarcasm. "To recap." "You said your

parents died, and you witnessed their murder." "As well as, your brother dying, two years ago."

"Yea, so." Namira says, with an attitude.

"So." Dr Benson says. Letting out a sigh. "I'm concerned about, your response to his death." "I don't

think, you have had the chance, to grieve."

"What do you mean?" Namira asks. Confused by what Dr Benson, is saying.

"You haven't had the chance, to process the death of your brother." Dr Benson responds.

"So, me trying to kill myself." Namira says. "Has to do with my brother's death?" She says, making

sure. She heard Dr Benson, correctly.

"In a way." Dr Benson replies. "Let me ask you this?" She says, closing her notes. "Did you seek

therapy, after these two incidents?"

"I went to therapy, when my parents died." Namira responds. "But when my brother died." Namira says, with a sigh. "I-I didn't think I needed it." She says, shrugging her shoulders. "I just dealt with it."

"My point exactly." Dr Benson says, with enthusiasm. "Based on what you have told me." She says. Continuing with, what she has to say. "The type of relationship." "That you, and *Jah* have developed."

"What you mean." Namira says, getting upset. "The type of relationship?!" She says. "He asked me to marry him" showing her, the seven-caret ring.

"Can you honestly say, that Jahmere loves you." Dr Benson says sternly. Looking Namira, directly in her face.

"What the fuck type of questions, are these!" Namira says, with irritation. "First, you trying to question, my best friend loyalty." Namira says, with a scoff. " Now, you trying to make me question, my nigga!" She says, getting up.

"I'm not trying, to make you do anything." Dr Benson says calmly. "Just take a seat please."

"I just want to go the fuck home." Namira says, sadly. "I just want, my life back." She says with exhaustion, sitting back on the couch.

"If you can agree." Dr Benson says. "To continue, these sessions." She says, closing her notebook. "I will let the hospital know." "That you can be released." She says, with a smile.

"Yea whatever." Namira says, getting up from her chair.

Release Day

Jahmere is right there, when Namira walks out the facility. She feels, as if she can breathe again.

Namira gets in the car, and is greeted with. Three dozen, white and red roses. "Aww baby, thank you." She says, putting her purse in the back seat. "Baby what's in the bags?" Noticing the Saks, and Neiman Marcus bags. Sitting in the backseat of the car, Jahmere doesn't say anything. He just continues to drive. She grabs one of the bags, and inside is purses. From Gucci to Chanel. Even Lou and Fendi- all her favorite designers. "Baby what." She says, notices this big ass box, with a bow on it.

Namira grabs it from the back seat. She puts it in her lap, and opens it. Inside is this, beautiful gold, and black dress. "Omg baby!" "*Donna Karen*, what all this for?" Namira asks.

Jahmere starts laughing. "This is for us, tonight." He says. "I gotta secure this connect, in New York." Jahmere says, putting his signals on. "They having a business dinner." So that he can, merge into the next lane. "I want you to come." Namira continues, looking inside the bags, she notices a couple pair of shoes. The gold leaf Giuseppe heels. The limited-edition Louboutin's, in black. "I asked Lee to pick out some stuff, for you." Jahmere says smiling.

"That's my bish." Namira says. "She knows, all the fly shit." "Matter fact." She says dialing her number.

"Hey sis." Leelee says, answering the phone. Sitting at the nailery station, drying her nail.

"Omg, bitch!" Namira says, admiring the designer items, in the bag smiling. "What you doing?"

"I'm in the nailery." Leelee responds. Looking at her chrome nails, checking to see if they are dry.

"Which one?" Namira asks, looking over at Jahmere. "I'm tell him to drop me off."

"You know, I only go to Nailpro." Leelee says, with a scoff.

"I need, mines done too." Namira says, looking at her growing nails. "You driving, sis?" She asks.

"Duh, sis." Leelee says. As if, Namira should already know.

"Bitch, I'm just asking." Namira says. She hanging up, the phone. "Can you drop me off, in South-

Philly?"

"I wanted to spend time with you." Jahmere says, sucking his teeth. "Buts it cool tho." He says, getting

off the exit toward South Philly.

"Leelee going drop me home." Namira says, as she gets out the car.

"Ard baby, enjoy yourself." Jahmere says. Giving Namira, two crisp, hundred-dollar bills. Giving her a

kiss, and speeding off.

Namira walks in the nailery, and she sees Leelee. She is sitting in the chair, getting her toes done.

"Aye!" Leelee says, loudly. "My bitch she out."

"You already know." Namira says, walking up to the chair. She sits down, right next to Leelee.

Namira takes off, her shoes. Ming, the manicurist, comes and runs her water. She puts her feet, in the water. It feels so good.

"We gotta get your hair done." Leelee says, looking at Namira messy bun.

"I don't got time." Namira says, sighing. "Jah talking about, he wants to leave, by eight." She says, rolling her eyes.

"He is irking." Leelee says, rolling her eyes. "Bah said the same thing." Namira and Leelee, continue to catch up. They leave the nail salon, and Leelee continue their conversation in the car. "You know, I did it so you can heal Mira." Leelee says, breaking the awkward silence.

"Yea, I know sis." Namira says, letting out a sigh. "I just." She begins to say. "I'm just trying to figure stuff out." "I'm pregnant, and then the shit with Jahmere."

"I get it sis." Leelee says. "I just don't want you trying to hurt yourself." Leelee says in a worried tone.

"I'm not sis." Namira says. "I'm taking it day, by day." She says, almost believing the lie. She still cant. Shake what Dr Benson said.

Chapter 5

Namira goes into her bedroom, so she can get ready. She sees that Jahmere left the bags, by the bed. She runs the shower first, it feels good to be home. Namira steps in the shower, and lets the steam relax her body. She takes her time showering, thinking about what Dr Benson said. Her mind begins to drift to her brother. Namira lets out a sigh, before turning the water off. She gets out the shower, and grabs a towel. She walks into her bedroom, grabbing her favorite lotion, *Donna Karen Cashmere*. Namira sits on the bed, so she can lotion up her body. She decides to wear. A lace push up bra, with the matching thong panties.

Namira gets a text from Jahmere, saying he is on his way. She doesn't have time, to get her hair done. So, she just tightens and retracts her weave. Styling her hair with big Kim Kardashian curls, to complement the style of the dress. Just when she is finishing, applying her makeup. In walks Jahmere, looking fly as ever. He has on his Prada shoes, in gray. A double-breasted tuxedo, in black. With a peach tie, just to give a pop, of color. "You ain't ready yet?" Jahmere says, stopping mid-sentence. "Damn." He says, walking over to her, gently grabbing her by her waist. Namira turns around, and she smiles. "Don't start." She can't get over, how fine he is. "You want us to be there, at a certain time." Namira says, as Jahmere picks her up, and kisses her. "Baby put me down." She says, in a playful tone. Fighting for Jahmere, to put her down. "Stop playing, we gotta go." Namira says. As Jahmere backs her up, against the balcony window.

The city lights are glowing behind them, through the blinds. Namira looks at him, with this hunger in her eyes. She begins, to unbuckle his pants. Namira can feel his hard dick, peeking through his pants. She smiles and says. "Damn." Namira says. "I missed this." Jahmere lifts one of her legs. Sliding her thong to the side, he enters Namira slowly. They both let out this moan, of satisfaction. Wrapping her leg around his waist. As he thrust deeper, inside of her. Namira can't help but to moan, out in pleasure.

"Shit Mira!" Jahmere says. As her wetness coats his dick. His phone starts ringing, but he just let his ring. He trying to concentrate.

"Damn Jah!" Namira moans out. Griping his shoulders tighter. "Baby we gotta stop." She says, looking in his eyes. "We already late." Namira says, kissing his juicy lips. They hear the locks, to the door turn, and in walks Leelee.

"If ya'll two don't-" She says, yelling through the condo. Heading toward, their bedroom. "Aww shit my bad!" Leelee says, covering her eyes. Walking right back out, their bedroom. Namira now regrets, giving Leelee a spare key. Jahmere goes in the bathroom and fixes himself. "Ya'll in here being nasty!" Leelee yells, from the living room.

"Bitch, yes!" Namira says. Irritated that Leelee interrupted them. She changes her panties, and hurries up to get dressed. Namira checks her hair, in the mirror. Jahmere didn't mess her curls up, too bad. She checks her make up, and it is still intact. She slips on her dress, and grabs her clutch. Namira asks Leelee, to zip up the back of the dress. Jahmere comes out the bedroom.

They all head down stairs, and get in the limo. Namira cannot stop smiling, she has to admit. It feels good to be home. It's just for some reason. She can't seem to get Dr Benson words, out of her head. Namira is not going, let that stop her, from having a good time. They arrive at the airport strip, where a jet is waiting for them. Namira and Jahmere, have their own private section. That separates them from, Leelee and Bahshere. Their hostess asks, if they would like anything to drink. Namira requests, a lemon water with cucumbers. Jahmere orders a shot of, Crown Royal. "Baby." Namira says, wanting to know the truth. "Is there something, you need to tell me? Namira asks. Looking directly in Jahmere eyes.

"What you talking about Mira." Jahmere says, with a confused look on his face.

"Just exactly what the fuck I said!" Namira says, snapping at him.

"Calm down what's wrong?" Jahmere asks, sitting next to her and grabbing her hand.

"Nothing." Namira says, with a sigh. She isn't trying to argue, and ruin the evening. She just can't seem to shake, what Dr Benson said to her earlier.

"Naw it gotta be something." Jahmere says. "The way you, snapping on me." He says caressing her hand. The hostess comes back, with their drinks. Namira guzzles her drink down. "Can I have another?" She asks. "This time more cucumbers please." Namira says, giving her a fake smile.

"Sure thing." The hostess says, taking Namira glass. So, she can refill it.

"I mean you lied to me about you, and." Namira begins to explain.

"Baby how many times." Jahmere says. "We going keep talking about, the bullshit." He says interrupting her.

"Jah, I am carrying your baby." Namira says. "Let's not forget." Dr Benson words, are starting to gnaw at her conscience. "I don't want you leaving me, for somebody else." "Or you going back to that bitch Shay."

Jahmere sucks his teeth. "Come on Mira." He says, grabbing her hands. "Can we stop talking about, irrelevant shit." Jahmere says, getting irritated. "Let's enjoy the rest, of the night." Jahmere says, kissing her on the lips. Namira has to admit, Jahmere is right. She just feels, something is not right.

Namira pushes the negative thoughts, out of her mind. She smiles and sits back. The hostess comes back, with her drink. Namira takes a sip and looks out the window. Enjoying the night that is ahead of her. They arrive at their private airport strip, and the limo is waiting for them. Jahmere helps Namira into the limo. "Baby you good?" He asks, noticing how quiet, she has been.

"Yes baby." Namira says, kissing him. "I'm okay." She says, looking out the window. Namira is just

trying to remain calm. She stares, out the window. Letting her mind drift, getting lost in the New York,

city lights. They arrive at this upscale restaurant. Located in the upper eastside of Manhattan called,

Daniel. She and Leelee wait, while they check on their reservation. "Bitch do you see this place."

Namira says.

Jahmere and Bahshere come back, and get them. The host leads them, to their dining area.

Which, is the *Bellecour Room*. It has grey leather accents, and mirrors. With ceramic tile accents, in the

corners of the room. Namira notices, some of Jahmere and Bahshere associates. They are here, with

their wives, and she recognizes one of them. "Jazmine!" Namira says, walking over to her, so she can

give her a hug.

"Omg, Namira!" Jazmine says. "How are you." She says, giving her a hug back. "I haven't seen you in

years."

"I've been good." Namira says smiling. "I'm getting married." She says, showing her the ring. She

notices Jahmere. Walking over to her, and she smiles. "Baby." She says, gently grabbing his arm. "I

want to introduce you to a friend of mine."

"Aww shit!" Jahmere says with a chuckle. "What up Jaz." He says, giving her a hug. "You taking care

of my brother?" Soon as Jahmere says that. His brother walks right up to him. Namira thought for a

second, she was seeing double.

"Wait, hold the fuck up." Namira says. "Ya'll twins?"

"Naw, we get that a lot tho." Jahmere says laughing. "I told you, I had a brother baby." He says, kissing her cheek.

"Yea, it's just ya'll could be twins." Namira says. *"Damn, he fine too."* She says, to herself. They both have the same features. Smooth caramel skin, almond shaped eyes, and nice straight white teeth. Only difference, is that Jahmere brother. He has a dimple in his left cheek, but Jahmere doesn't. Namira notices Leelee walking up. "Best friend!" "I-"

"I know who this tramp is." Leelee says, rolling her eyes and moving past them. Taking a seat, next to Bahshere. Jazmine rolls her eyes, as she takes a seat, as the men get reacquainted. The wives, make chit chatter among themselves.

Namira excuses herself, so she can use the bathroom. Just when she is, about to come out the stall. She hears two voices, and they mention Va'Shay. "Damn." One of the females, voices says. "I guess, he really done with Shay, dusty ass." Namira recognizes, one of the voices as Jazmines.

"You know she slept with, half of his friends up here." The female voice says. Fixing her hair, in the mirror. "Get this, her and Jah was never married." She says, with a smirk on her face. "She never filed, for the marriage certificate."

"Wait, wait." Jazmine says. "How do you know, all this?" She says. Wanting her to spill more, of this tea.

"My hairdresser is friends with her." The female says, with a smirk. "Rumor is, she was and *still is,* sleeping with Bahshere, around the time he got book." She says, washing her hands and grabbing the hand towel. "Ooh girl, wait until I tell Quin!" Jazmine says, referring to Jahmere brother.

"Bitch is you crazy." She says, to Jazmine. "I not getting, in the middle of this drama." She says, rolling her eyes. "So, keep ya big mouth shut." She says, as they both, leave out of the bathroom.

Namira feels, her heart has been ripped, out of her chest. She really can't believe, what she just heard. Her blood begins to boil. What is making her angry, is that they're not even married. She is pacing back and forth, in the bathroom. Having a conversation with herself. *"He really must think, that I am the fuck stupid."* Namira is trying to calm herself, so she won't cause a scene. If what she just discovered, is true. Why is he still dealing with Va'Shay? If their marriage is really over?

"He must be still fucking her." Namira says to herself. As she checks, her make up in the mirror. She quickly wipes them away, as she leaves out the bathroom. Namira goes back into the dining area. So, she can find Jahmere. She sees him talking, to a group of niggas. They are talking shit, and smoking on cigars. Namira marches directly, over to him.

Jahmere notices Namira walking over to him. "Hey baby, I want to introduce." Namira smacks him across the face. Not caring, that she is causing a scene. "Aye yo!" Jahmere says, in disbelief.

"You a fucking liar!" Namira says, with anger in her voice. "This whole time, you were lying to me!" She says, yelling at him.

"Calm down, yo." Jahmere says. Pulling her off to the side. "Lower your voice." He says, noticing that people are starting to stare. Leelee walks over to them. She saw the whole thing happen. When she was having, a conversation with Bahshere. "Aye sis, you good?"

"Don't touch me Lee." Namira says, snatching her arm away. "How long you knew." She says, cutting her eyes at her. "This, motherfucker ain't married!" Namira says, raising her voice. "Yea, I overheard the conversation in the bathroom." She says, turning to Jahmere. "She never filed for the marriage certificate." Namira says, folding her arms. Waiting for Jahmere to say something.

"Sis, the fuck is you talking about?" Leelee says. Really confused, as to what is going on. Namira ignores Leelee, turning her attention to Jahmere, and says. "That's why you kept jerking me around?" She says, demanding an answer. "You lied to me Jah!" Namira says, storming off. She hates to admit this, but her therapist was right.

"I fucking asked you!" Namira says, pointing her finger, in his chest. "Was there anything, you had to tell me!" Namira takes off the ring, and throws it at him. "I'm fucking done!" She leaves out the restaurant, and flags down a taxi.

Namira has to get away from Jahmere. It starting to become too overwhelming. Jahmere is calling after her, rushing over to the taxi. Grabbing the door, before it closes. He gets in and says "baby I'm telling you-" He begins to explain, but Namira cuts him off.

"No!" Namira yells, not evening want him to talk to him. "Just, stop talking to me please." The cab driver looks at Namira, through the rearview mirror. "You made a fool of me tonight." She says, looking out the window. "Why do you keep hurting me?" Namira isn't mad, that he isn't married. The issue is, for the past year and half, that they been together. Jahmere treated their relationship, like if it wasn't exclusive. Making her feel, that she was the other women. The taxi pulls into some traffic, Namira notice's a bar on the corner. She tells the driver to stop, and she gets out of the taxi. Walking into the bar.

"Namira baby hold up." Jahmere says. Paying the taxi driver and jogging after her. He follows Namira into the bar. He sees the bartender, place a martini in front of her. Jahmere walks up to the bar, and pushes the glass, away from Namira. "Chill, can we just talk, please."

"You been lying to me!" Namira says, in an angry tone. "You were never married!"

"I swear, I don't-" That when Jahmere stops. He remembers when he asked Va'Shay, for the marriage certificate. So, he could continue, with the separation. Every time he asked Va'Shay about it. She would make up a bullshit ass story, about how she couldn't find it. "I fucking love you girl." Jahmere says, with seriousness in his voice. "Why can't you see that?"

"Ohh, I don't know." Namira says, with sarcasm. "You have this nut ass baby mom." "Like check *that*

bitch Jah." She says with an attitude. "You asked *me* to marry *you*." Jahmere is not afraid of Va'Shay.

It's about the drama, that she will cause in his life. He takes a deep breath, before speaking. "Look

Mira-"

"I just want you Jah." Namira says with a sigh, interrupting him. "I feel you not fully committed to me,

or this relationship." She says, with a sigh. "I want all of you, not parts of you." Jahmere has to admit,

Namira is right. Things are going to be hard though. He just doesn't want, things to get out of hand.

Plus, it's just a matter of time, before Namira finds out. Va'Shay is the one, behind Say'Von murder.

He snaps out of his own thoughts, and says. "Ard, well let's get the fuck outta here." Jahmere says,

helping Namira down off the bar stool.

Jahmere flags down a cab. He helps Namira get into the cab. Jahmere gives the driver, the address to

the hotel. She rests her head against, Jahmere's chest and she drifts to sleep. He pulls out his phone,

and he has a text from Bahshere. He wants to know, if everything is cool. Jahmere replies back, and

asks about the connect. Bahshere texts back, telling him that they got it. Jahmere closes his phone,

enjoying the rest of the ride. He takes a deep breath, because it's going to be some shit, when they back

to Philly.

The cab driver pulls up, to the entrance of the hotel. Jahmere wakes up Namira, and helps her get out of the cab. They walk into the hotel. Taking the elevator to their penthouse suite. That has a view, overlooking the city. They order some room service. So, they can enjoy each other's company. They both fall asleep. Namira is awaken, by Jahmere's phone ringing. She tries her best, to ignore it and let it ring. But her curiosity, gets the best of her. Namira decides to answer, as she creeps away from Jahmere. It's a FaceTime, from an unrecognized number. Namira heads into the bathroom. She answers the video call. "Where the fuck is Jah" Va'Shay says, rolling her eyes.

"What do you want." Namira says. Trying not to lose her cool, and cuss her scheming ass the fuck out.

"Bitch." Va'Shay says in a commanding tone. "Put my husband on the phone." She says in an irritated tone.

Namira starts to laugh. "Ya husband, bitch you fucking delusional." She says, laughing at her. "Ya trifling ass didn't, even go and file for a marriage certificate." Namira says rolling her neck and giving her attitude. "You pinning kids on *my fiancé*." Namira says, flashing her ring and laughing. "Those kids not even his."

"Says the bitch, who tried to kill herself." Va'Shay says with a quickness. "Didn't you lose one of the babies?" She says, with a cackle. "What type of crazy shit is that."

Namira blood starts to boil, but she not going give Va'Shay, the satisfaction. "You fucking delusional." She says, pacing back, and forth in the bathroom. "You thought them kids would keep him." She says laughing. "They not even his, wait till he finds this shit out." Namira says, with venom in her voice. She hangs up the phone and smiles. Thinking that she won the battle. Then she wonders, how the fuck. Va'Shay know, about her being in the hospital. She walks out the bathroom, to confront Jahmere for answers.

"Baby, you seen my phone." Jahmere says, turning towards Namira. He notices that she has his, phone in her hand. "*Shit.*" Jahmere thinks to himself, as he walks up to Namira.

"You told that bitch, about what happened?!" Namira says, throwing the phone at him.

Jahmere ducks, and his phone breaks against the wall. "Whoa." "Calm the fuck down."

"Don't tell me to calm down." Namira says, walking up to Jahmere. "Why you telling that bitch, about us." She says. "You be pillow talking with this hoe, about me." Namira says, mushing Jahmere in his face.

Jahmere grabs her by her waist. "Why you stressin about a bitch, I'm not with anymore." He says, pulling her closer to him. "Mira come on yo." He says with pleading eyes. "A nigga trying yo. Jahmere says, kissing her. "Let me get you out this dress." He says kissing her on her neck.

Chapter 6

"Naw, you ain't getting no pussy tonight." Namira says. Pushing him off of her, and walking towards the bathroom. She stops near the doorway. "Are you joining me?" She says, zipping down her dress. Letting it drop to the floor. Going into the bathroom, and running the shower. Jahmere licks his lips, he begins to get undress, so he can join Namira in the shower. He walks into the bathroom, admiring her frame, through the glass door. From her phat ass and plump breast. It turns him on, and his dick starts to get hard. "Baby is you going to just stand there." Namira says, opening the shower door. "Or are you going to join me."

Jahmere gets in the shower, and the water is hot. He backs her up, against the glass shower door. Kissing Namira passionately. Caressing her body, making her want him more. He cups her breast and begins to suck on her nipples, one at a time. Sending a tingling sensation through her body. He takes two fingers, an enters them into her pussy. "Damn baby, ya shit wet as fuck." He says kissing her lips, and turning Namira around. Jahmere enters Namira from the back. He grips the sides of her waist. As the water dances off each other bodies. She just looks back at him. He continues to thrust inside of her, making her pussy wetter. The water begins to turn cold, letting them know. That it's time, to get out the shower.

Namira gets out the shower and grabs a towel. She turns around and Jahmere is standing, right in front of her. The water is just glistening off his body. Running down his chest and back. He puts her on top of the sink, kissing his way down to her pussy. Lifting one of her legs and putting it on his shoulder. "Damn Jah." She says, looking down at him. Jahmere looks up at her, while he is eating her pussy. It's something about the way he is staring at her. While he is eating her out. That turns her on, even more. She arches her back. Allowing Jahmere to get better access, to her clit and slit. Pushing the back of his head, deeper between her legs. As she feels an orgasm beginning to build. Namira grips the edge of the sink. "Ohh s-s-shiit." She moans out. Allowing her juices to flow in his mouth.

"Mmm." Jahmere says. Slurping and licking every drop. Her legs are shaking. As this euphoric sensation, takes over her body. Jahmere comes up and picks her up. He carries her to the bed, and lays her down. The moonlight hits her body, in all the right places. Jahmere climbs, on top of her. Namira just smiles, and pulls him closer to her. Jahmere enters inside of her. "Damn ya shit wet as fuck." He says, pumping into her slow and steady. Namira wraps her legs around him. As his pace, begins to pick up. "Jah, baby I love you."

"You love me, huh." Jahmere says, with a smirk. As he continues, to stroke inside of her. He turns Namira over, and she arches her back. Her ass bounces, against his dick. He pulls her hair, with each strong stroke. Jahmere asks "who pussy is this."

"It's your baby!" Namira yells out, in pleasure. "It's yours!" She moans, as he hitting her g-spot. The better Namira arches, her back. The deeper Jahmere goes inside of her.

"Oh shit, I'm about to nut!" Jahmere yells out. Gripping her waist, thrusting inside of her, even more. Namira can feel another orgasm, beginning to form. "I'm about to cum!" She yells, before they both cum, together. Collapsing on the bed. Trying to catch their breaths.

Jahmere kisses Namira, on her forehead, watching as Namira drifts to sleep. He has to make things right. For the sake of their child. As well as, their relationship. Jahmere knows, he is going to have to tell Namira. That he knows about who was involved, in her brother getting murdered. It's just that he needs more time. This is not the right time, especially with Namira being pregnant. He doesn't want to stress her out even more. Jahmere isn't being insensitive to what she is saying. It's just, Va'Shay is not going to let him go easy. If she got Say'Von set up, and killed. What else, is she capable of. That is something, he is not going to take a chance on. Or putting his baby at risk. Jahmere looks over at Namira, as she sleeps in his arms. He can't help, but to smile. It just he feels bad, that he keeping a secret from her.

Two Months Later

"Baby don't forget." Namira says, coming out the bathroom. "We find out what the sex, of the baby today." She says, coming out of the bathroom.

"Aww shit." Jahmere says. Forgetting the appointment was today.

"What." Namira says, getting annoyed. "Don't tell me, you can't come."

"Naw, I'm be there." Jahmere says getting up. He grabs his phone out the living room. Texting Bahshere, about the meet up.

"Yea okay?" Namira asks. As she finishes, getting ready for work.

Jahmere comes in the bedroom. "I know you not mad, at me Mira." He says, noticing her getting an attitude.

"You better be there Jah." Namira says, turning around to him. Jahmere smiles, seeing her little belly poking out under her dress. "You look good." Jahmere says, giving her a kiss on her cheek.

"Well, how am I supposed to look." Namira responds, rolling her eyes. "Ugly and fat."

"Aye yo, ya attitude is outta pocket." Jahmere says, shaking his head. Gripping her up playfully and kissing her lips.

"You going make me late." Namira says, letting out a small laugh. As she goes, into her walk-in closet. Trying to figure out, what pair of pumps she should wear. Her Lou's, or her Manolo's. She decides, on her Manolo nude pumps. Namira checks herself out, in the full-length mirror. She looks at her growing baby bump. Namira rubs her stomach and smiles. "Okay baby I'm heading to work." She says, walking into the living room. Namira grabs her keys, and her purse. Giving Jahmere a kiss.

"Daddy loves you." Jahmere says, to her belly.

Namira smiles and leaves out. Her phone starts to ring, as she is heading towards her car. She looks at the caller id, and it's Leelee. She hasn't spoken to her. Since the incident, back in New York. Namira is starting to distance herself from her. As Namira is walking up, to her car. She sees, all four of her tires. Are slashed, on her Lexus Coupe. "The fuck!?" She says, calling Jahmere. "Baby, can you take me to work." She says, letting a sigh of frustration. "Somebody slashed my fucking tires."

"Here I come." Jahmere says, rushing off the phone. About five minutes later, he comes down to the parking lot. "Ohh shit." He says, walking up to her car. "Look I'm get it fixed for you." Jahmere says. As they walk, over to his Benz. "I'm have Leelee, drop your car off."

Namira makes this face. "Jah stop fucking playing with me." She says, getting in the car. "I don't fuck with her, sneaky ass."

"Mira, stop being petty." Jahmere says, starting up the car and pulling out the parking garage. "Ya'll been best friends, for how long." Jahmere asks, sarcastically. Trying to get Namira to see, their friendship is bigger. Then their little misunderstanding.

"What that got to do with anything." Namira says. "I'm starting to feel I can't trust her now."

"Aww baby, don't be like that." Jahmere says. "Just hear, what she has to say." He suggests, trying to get Namira to understand. Making a left on Spruce Street, and double parking the Benz. He puts his hazards on. So, the cars can know to go around him. "At least think about it." Jahmere says, trying to be the peacemaker.

"Ohh and I think it's time for a car upgrade." Namira says, switching the subject.

Jahmere starts laughing. "If you can put ya differences, to the side." "Then maybe I'll get you a Toyota."

"A Toyota!" Namira says. "Jah don't play with me." She says, sucking her teeth. "Just for that, I want the new Range Rover."

"I'm think about it." Jahmere says, as he pulls off.

"Whatever." Namira says, sticking up her middle finger, as she walks into her job. *"Namira's Interior Décor."* She heads up, to her office. Her secretary, Ashely greets her. "Ya eight-thirty, is here." She says, handing Namira a cup, of decaffeinated green tea, as Namira heading into her office.

"Good morning." She says, greeting her client. "My apologies, for the last meeting we had." She says, sitting her tea on the table.

"Ohh no problem, Ms. Wilson." Her client says, with a smile.

They finish discussing, the details for her client's wedding. Namira walks her out her office, and over to the elevators. Advising her to call her, if she has any more questions. She heads back to her office, and takes a seat at her desk. Namira looks at the view of the city, and rubs her belly. She watches the cars move, through the city. Namira looks at the diamond ring, on her left hand. Everything that she has been, asking for from Jahmere. It's starting to come into formation. Her phone begins to ring, interrupting her thoughts. She looks at the caller id. *Leelee* flashes, across the screen. Namira rolls her eyes and answers. "Hello." She says, dryly.

"Hey, wassup girl." Leelee says, in a cheerful tone. "I been calling you." She says with hesitancy. "You haven't been returning my calls."

"No, this bitch didn't." Namira says to herself. *"Did she forget what happened in New York." "She got some fucking nerve."*

"Jah wanted me to bring you your car." Leelee says. Sensing the distance, in her voice. "Cause its ready."

"I'll see when you get here." Namira says, hanging up. She can't even deal with. The bullshit with Leelee, right now. Her phone rings again. This time its Jahmere. She answers. "Hey baby."

"What time, is the appointment?" Jahmere asks.

"Three o'clock at Pennsylvania." Namira says, rubbing her belly. "Please don't be late."

"Mira." Jahmere says, with seriousness in his voice. "Yo, dead this shit!" He says, hanging up on her. Namira is about to call Jahmere back. So, she can cuss him out, but Leelee is calling her again. "Hello." Namira answers, rolling her eyes.

"I'm on my way up." Leelee says, as she walks into the building. Pushing the button, for the elevator. About five minutes later. Leelee walks in her office "hey girl." She says, sitting in a chair. Namira doesn't say anything, she gets up and walks over to Leelee. "Omg, girl look at that belly." She says, going into her Chanel purse, to get the keys. "Aww that my god baby." Leelee says, rubbing Namira's belly.

"Wait hold." Namira says, taking a step back. "We not cool." She says, crossing her arms. You didn't tell me that wasn't married." Namira says, walking towards her desk. "I heard the conversation in the bathroom." "When we were in New York."

"I really don't know." Leelee says, with a scoff. "What you talking about."

"You, ain't know, Jah and Shay really not married?" Namira asks, walking up to Leelee.

"You fucking lying!" Leelee says laughing. "Wait till, I tell Bah this shit." She says, pulling out her phone and dialing his number. "Wait." "That's why, you been ducking my calls." She says, in disbelief. "Cause this mess over Shay?" Leelee asks, walking up to Namira. "I honestly didn't know." She says, looking Namira in her eyes.

"It's just that when I was in the-" Namira stops mid-sentence. "Never mind, sis." Namira says hugging her. "It's just I missed you that all." She can feel the tears, forming in the corner of her eyes.

"What the matter Mira?" Leelee asks. Grabbing two tissues, from off her desk.

"Nothing." Namira says, chuckling. "It's just my hormones."

"Well let's go get some lunch." Leelee suggest.

"Sure, we need to catch up anyway." Namira says, grabbing her purse and keys. They get on the elevator, and they walk out the building. Namira and Leelee get into her car. Namira, catches Leelee up. "What's going on, with you and Bah?" Namira asks. Making a right, onto 18th and Rittenhouse Square.

"I think he is cheating on me again." Leelee says, letting out a sigh.

"Bitch!" Namira says, as she pulls into a parking spot. "With who?" She says, giving her that look. They get out of Namira's car, and she puts money in the meter. Heading into *Devon Seafood, and Grille*. Namira and Leelee wait for the host, to seat them.

"I don't know." Leelee says. "Every time I try to fuck him, he wanna get an attitude. "Or, telling me he

too tired." She says. This isn't the first time. Leelee had to deal, with Bahshere infidelity issues.

The host comes up, interrupting Leelee. "Hello my name is Sam." He says, smiling. "Would you like to

sit near the bar?" "Or the patio section?"

"Can we get the patio." Namira says to the host, as he shows them to their seats. He sits the menus on

the table, and walks way.

"Like I was saying." Leelee says, continuing their conversation. "He never turns down sex, or head."

She says sitting her Chanel clutch, on the table.

"What, you going to do?" Namira says. Wasting no time, looking at the menu.

"Nothing yet." Leelee says, looking at the menu. "I have no proof." She says, letting out a sigh. "We

always arguing." She continues to explain. "We not having no angry sex." "Shit fucking annoying."

Namira starts laughing. It reminds her of how, her and Jahmere use to be.

The waiter takes their orders. As usual, Leelee orders a Margarita and a shot of Jack Daniels. Namira

just get a sparking lemon water. The waiter goes to put in their orders. "How does it feel being

pregnant?" Leelee asks, switching the topic.

"I'm ready for the baby to come." Namira says, rubbing her belly. "We go to see what the sex is,

today." Namira says, smiling.

"Call me later today. Leelee says. "I have a marketing meeting, later today." She says, checking her phone.

About a half hour, later their food comes out. Namira orders, the lemongrass shrimp tacos. Leelee orders, the Lobster mac and cheese, with the truffle bread crumbs. "This food looks good." Namira says, wasting no time to eating.

"Ya pregnant ass, I swear." Leelee says, laughing.

They continue with their conversation. Va'Shay walks in, with her loud. Ghetto talking ass. Namira peeps, and she rolls her eyes. She is trying to remain calm, and not go off on her. Leelee peeps Namira vibe. She looks in Namira's direction. "The fuck." She says with a look, of disgust. "Is this bitch, following us or what."

"Bitch, I don't know." Namira says, waving over the waiter. "But I'm ready to go." They pay for their food, and purposely walk past, Va'Shay table. Namira flips her hair. Throwing her Lou purse, over her arm.

 "Yea, that her stupid ass." Va'Shay starts laughing. "You having fun, with my leftovers."

"You never had Jah, in the first place." Namira says, with a smirk. Leelee is standing right by Namira side, just in case anything pops off. "Why every time, I see ya ghetto goofy ass." Namira says. "You got all this shit to say." She says, getting in Va'Shay face.

"Mira, chill out you pregnant." Leelee says, grabbing her arm.

"I don't give a fuck!" Namira says. Pulling her arm, away from Leelee. "I'm having his baby and I'm be his wife." She says yelling. "In *Real life* bitch, not just for play." Namira says, showing off the engagement ring.

Va'Shay gets up from the table. She comes charging towards Namira, grabbing Namira by her hair. Va'Shay friend, comes and tries to jump in the fight. Leelee, pulls the girl off. Punching her all in her face. The store owner comes over, to see what is the commotion. He threatens to call the cops, if they don't stop fighting. People are starting to stare. Namira is trying to block, Va'Shay from hitting her. One of those hits' lands in Namira stomach. All she can think about, is her baby. The store owner comes, and breaks up the fight. Order them to leave, and the cops have been called. Va'Shay's friend is dragging Shay out. "I hope ya baby die!" She yells. "This shit is not the fuck over!"

Leelee, rushes over to Namira. "Mira, you cool." Namira can feel this warm sensation, between her legs. She looks down and she is bleeding.

"Sis call Jah." Namira says, in a worried tone. "I don't want to lose my baby." The store owner comes up, and sees Namira bleeding. "I'm call 911!" He says rushing, to grab the phone. Leelee gets her phone out her purse. She dials Jahmere number.

Chapter 7

"Yo sis." Jahmere says, answering on the first ring. The paramedics rush in the restaurant. Placing Namira, on the stretcher. They tell Leelee, they are going to take her to Pennsylvania hospital.

"Meet me at Pennsylvania." Leelee say quickly. "It's Mira." Leelee says hanging up. She grabs their food, and gets in Namira's car. She parks the car, and heads into Pennsylvania hospital.

Namira is going in and out. Her vision is blurry, all she can see is blurry figures over her. "Ms. Wilson can you hear me?" The nurse asks, trying to see if she is responsive. The nurse checks her pupils, they are starting to dilate. They get her hooked up to a heart monitor. Putting an ultrasound, around her belly. So, they can check, the baby heartbeat. Her body starts to crash, and she starts to shake violently. "I need a doctor in her now!" The nurse yells…...

In the Waiting room

Leelee is pacing back and forth. "God please." She says, looking up to the ceiling. Her phone starts to ring. She answers the call, without even looking at the caller id. "Jah where the hell-"

"I hope that bitch baby dies!" Va'Shay says, with so much venom.

"I swear, I'm kill you myself." Leelee says, screaming through the phone. She doesn't care, that she is in the hospital. "I hate the fact, I called ya trifling ass." "My sister." Leelee spits back. Meaning every word, that she is saying.

"Same here bitch." Va'Shay says. "That's why, I'm still fucking Bahshere."

"Bitch say that shit again" Leelee says. Making sure, she heard this hoe correctly.

"I'm." Va'Shay says. "Fucking Bahshere." She says, popping her gum in her ear.

"I'm kill you." Leelee says. "You ain't gotta worry, about Jah doing it first." She says, hanging up.

Jahmere and Bahshere, come walking in the emergency room. They look like, they are ready to kill

somebody. "Lee, what happened." Jahmere says, with worry in his eyes.

As soon as Leelee sees Bahshere. She goes and smacks him, across the face. "You still fucking her!"

"The fuck is she talking about Bah!" Jahmere says. Not wanting to deal, with his bullshit either.

"Nigga, I don't know." Bahshere says calmly. "You know Shay always starting some shit." He says to

Jahmere. "Lee, chill the fuck out."

"Ain't no fucking chill." Leelee says, ready to go off. If it's true, then she going have to kill both of

them.

"Yo Lee, tell me what happened with Mira." Jahmere says in a worried voice.

"Well, me and her was at lunch earlier." Leelee begins to explain. "Then Shay-" Jahmere puts his hand

up. Signaling for Leelee to stop talking. "Don't tell me, Shay hoes ass the reason, Mira in the hospital!"

Jahmere say with frustration.

In the operating room…

The doctor checks the baby, on the ultra sound. It seems the placenta, has broken. "We are going to have to deliver this baby." He says, looking at the nurse. "I need her prepped, for an emergency C-section." "Now!" The doctor yells. They manage to stabilize Namira body. So, they can start the procedure, for the emergency C- section. Namira is losing a lot of blood. "I'm going to need a blood transfusion stat!" The doctor calls for the nurse. Ordering her, to transfer the baby to the NICU. They manage to get a heart-beat, but it is faint. Namira body begins to crash again. She is losing a lot of blood. Her heart beat stops.

Namira can hear, the faint voices of the doctors. But she keeps following the light. She sees the outline of a figure, as she gets closer. Namira she can tell who it is. "Omg!" She says runs up to him.

"Hey lil sis." Say'Von says smiling. Giving Namira a hug. "it's really me." He says chuckling, hugging her tightly. Namira just cries, she doesn't have any words. "I know, I know." Say'Von says. "I'm always with you." "Don't ever forget that." He says kissing her cheek.

"What happened that night." Namira says, really wanting to know. She always wanted to ask her brother. Now, she has the chance to know.

"Well." Say'Von says, beginning to tell what happened. "I remember Shay calling me and-"

"Wait, wait hold the fuck up." Namira says. "Shay as in Va'Shay?"

"Yea sis, that's Leelee older sister." Say'Von says. He continues to speak, but Namira can't hear what he is saying. A faint light begins to shine, and she is being pulled back into reality.

"I am getting a steady pulse." The doctor says, looking at the monitor. "Ms. Wilson can you hear me." The doctor asks. Namira opens her eyes, she is back into the hospital. "Ms. Wilson." The doctor says to her. "Just get some rest." Namira eyes began to close, as she drifts off to sleep. The conversation with her brother, keeps playing in her head. "All I remember, is Shay calling."

"Yea, sis Leelee and Shay are sisters."

Back In the waiting room

"Can ya'll shut the fuck up!" Jahmere yells, at Leelee and Bahshere. His head is starting to hurt, he cant believe that Namira is in the hospital. This time over Va'Shay trifling ass.

"My bad bro." Bahshere says. Forgetting that they in the hospital.

"If something happens to Mira and my baby." Jahmere says, pacing the floor.

"Aye yo bro, chill." Bahshere says, walking over to Jahmere. Trying to calm him down.

"Naw fuck that shit." Jahmere spits angrily. "Nigga, all this bullshit is because of Shay hoe ass." The doctor comes out, Jahmere rushes up to him. "Doctor how is she doing." He asks." Is the baby okay?"

The doctor takes a deep breath, before answering. "We had to deliver the baby early, because it was no way he-"

"Wait it's a boy!?" Leelee says, walking up to them. Interrupting the doctor.

"Yes." The doctor says. "He wouldn't have been able, to survive." "The placenta was broken beyond repair." He says. "So, we had to deliver him."

"He is in the NICU now." The doctors say, turning to Jahmere. "Upon delivery he suffered minor heart complications, but he is fine." He says to Jahmere, noticing his expression on his face.

"She lost a lot of blood." The doctor says. "Her body has gone through, a lot of shock." "She is doing fine now."

"Can I go in and see her?" Jahmere asks, just wanting to be with Namira.

"Yes of course." The doctor says. "Follow me." Jahmere follows the doctor, and so does Leelee and Bahshere.

"Where ya'll going?" Jahmere asks. Stopping them from stepping, any further. "Ya'll not going back there." Leelee sucks her teeth, and says "come on Jah."

"You heard what the fuck, I said." Jahmere says, in a serious tone. "You, and that hoe, have done enough." He says, with disgust in his voice. Giving Leelee, the death stare. He follows the doctor to Namira's room.

"You can go right in." The doctors say to Jahmere. "I have another patient to check on." He says, giving Jahmere a pat on the shoulder. "I will back shortly."

Jahmere walks into the room. Namira is hooked up, to all these machines and tubes. He walks up to her bed and grabs a chair. Jahmere sits next to her, grabbing her hand. He is trying to keep it all together. Jahmere lowers his head, as a tear runs down his face. The doctor comes in the room. Jahmere wipes the tears away." Where is my son?" Jahmere asks.

"He is in the NICU." The doctor says. "Would you like to see him?"

"Yea please." Jahmere manages to say, trying not to be emotional. The doctor leads Jahmere down, to the NICU department. They stop in front of the NICU window. The doctor explains to Jahmere, that his son. Must stay in the hospital, for the next couple months. Due to him being born early. Jahmere watches. As his son is hooked up, to all types of machines and IV's. "Aye yo doc." Jahmere says. "Can I please go in." He asks, with desperation. "I need to see, my son."

"Let me check with the nurse first." The doctors say, as he goes, and speaks with the nurse. The doctor then comes out, and gets Jahmere. He enters the NICU with caution. The nurse advises him to put on a smock. She tells him, to wash his hands with the medicated soap. After Jahmere does that, he walks up to the incubator. Jahmere watches, as the machines help his son breath. And monitor, keeps track of his heartbeat. All he can think about, is the condition Namira and his son is in.

Jahmere phone begins to ring. He looks down and the name *"Bah"* flashes. He slides the call to ignore. He calls again, and Jahmere answers it. "What yo!"

"Aye yo we got a situation!" Bahshere says, as his voice booms through the phone. "They raided the house and took all the product!"

The way Jahmere is feeling right now. He doesn't have time for the bullshit. "Ard, I'm coming." Jahmere looks at his son. "Aye lil man, daddy going be back." "You stay strong." He kisses the incubator and heads out the hospital.

On the drive home

"I'm so fucking done with you Bah!" Leelee says. "Fuck you!" She says, smacking him upside the head.

"Stop, hitting me, while I'm driving" Bahshere says, trying to concentrate on the road.

They drive in silence. Leelee is really trying to remain calm. She crosses her arms and looks out the window. Bahshere doesn't know what to say. He has to figure out a way, to control the damage. *"Why the fuck would she run her fucking mouth."* He says, to himself. *"She trying to fuck up everything."* Bahshere pulls into their home, in Roxborough. Leelee jumps out the car first. She goes in the house, upstairs to their bedroom.

"He thinks, I'm put up with his bullshit." Leelee says, heading to the walk-in closet. She snatches

Bahshere clothes, off the hangers. Throwing his sneakers and iced-out Rolex watches. Leelee smashes

them on the marble counters. Going into the bathroom and grabbing the bottle of bleach. *"He thinks*

I'm fucking playing." She says to herself. *"That I am a joke right."* Pouring the bleach all over his

clothes, and on his watches.

Bahshere is coming into the house. He can't believe Va'Shay would, run her mouth. He grabs his

phone, and sends Va'Shay a text, as he walks into the house. Bahshere can smell, a strong aroma of

bleach. "Aww shit!" He says, rushing up the steps. "Aye yo what the fuck are you doing?!"

"I told you the last time." Leelee says. Heading back, in the walk-in closet. "Don't fucking play with

me!" She yells, walking over to the pile of clothes, and see that they are ruined. "Baby, I'm telling you

the truth." Bahshere says walking into the closet. "I'm not fucking her!"

"Why would you do this to me!" Leelee yells. "I helped you with everything!" She says, as the tears

fall. "Get off me!" Leelee says, walking out the closet. She walks, over to her vanity. She opens the

drawer, grabbing her glock. Leelee told herself, that she is not going to continue. Tolerating Bahshere's

infidelities. She forgave him the last time, and he promised he change. Yet, here they are, dealing with

the same bullshit.

"Come on baby." Bahshere says, following after her. "You got." He stops mid-sentence. Leelee has the

gun, aimed at him.

"If it wasn't for me washing this money." Leelee says. "Investing it, and shit." "Then it would just be drug money." She says, sarcastically. "Like I said." She says, with the gun in her hand. "You got until the count of three." Bahshere backs out of the room. He hurries down the steps. Taking two, and three at a time. Bahshere slams the door, hopping in his Benz. Speeding off, he dials Jahmere number. Letting him know, he is on his way.

Leelee goes down stairs, to get a glass of wine. As she is heading back upstairs. She hears a knock, at the door. Leelee sits her wine glass, and the bottle of wine. On her dining room table, and head to the door. She looks through the peephole, and it's the cops. *"Shit."* Leelee says, to herself. She checks herself in the mirror, wiping the dried tears, from her face. Leelee takes a deep breath, and answers the door. "Good evening officers, can I help you."

"We got a call from your neighbor." The office says, chewing his gum. "Saying that she heard gunshots, coming from your home." He says. "Do you mind if we look around?" The other officer asks, breaking Leelee train of thought.

"No problem officers." Leelee says moving to the side. Letting the officers in. She says a silent prayer, as they look around.

"Okay ma'am." The officer says. "We don't suspect anything, out the usual." The officer says, as they leave. Leelee lets out a sigh of relief, as she grabs the bottle of wine. Taking her glass and heading back upstairs. She sits on the bed and pours herself some wine. Leelee begins to cry, because she is just over the bullshit. The lies and Bahshere just not, being faithful to her. It's time she let it all go. "Fuck him, it's his loss." She says to herself, pouring her another glass.

Pennsylvania Hospital

Every single day, Jahmere is at the hospital. Right by Namira and their son side. The doctors recommend, that Namira stay in the hospital a few more days. Their son, must stay for a few more months. Just until he is well developed. So he can eat and breath, without any assistance. Namira wakes up, as her eyes adjust to the lights. "Baby relax, he is okay." Jahmere says, trying to keep Namira calm. "They have him in the NICU."

"How long have I been here?" Namira asks, sitting up in the bed, trying to adjust the pillow behind her head. "I want to see my son!" Namira says in a demanding tone.

"You been here for about a week." Jahmere says. "I'm go get the nurse." He says, walking out the room. The nurse comes in with a wheel chair. He helps Namira into the wheel chair. The nurse places the IV, on the pole of the wheelchair. Jahmere holds her hand and they are led, to the NICU room. "There he is." Jahmere says, pointing through the glass window. "Would you like to see him?"

"Yes." Namira replies. As Jahmere wheels her, into the room. The caretaking nurse, advises Namira

and Jahmere. To wash their hands, and to put smocks on. "He is so little." Namira says, turning to

Jahmere. "Baby, I'm so sorry." She says, sadly. "This is all my fault."

"Naw it ain't." Jahmere says, kissing her on the cheek. "He is alive." He says, with reassurance. "That

is the most important part." Jahmere says, wiping the tears away. "I'm fix this shit." Jahmere says.

Hoping Namira would, believe the words he was saying.

Chapter 8

"Okay, Ms. Wilson." The doctor says, handing Namira her forms. "You are free to go home." Namira

signs her release papers. The nurse escorts her outside, in a wheelchair. She puts one her black Chanel

shades, as Jahmere's pull up. Double parking in the middle of the street. He hops out, looking sexy as

ever. Fresh Timbs, and his Balmain hoodie. His Caesar haircut and fresh trimmed goatee, was shaped

up to perfection. "Damn." Namira says, he jogs from the car. Walking up to Namira, helping her into

the passenger seat. He gets in, on the driver side. "Baby you look good as fuck." Jahmere just laughs,

and speeds through the downtown traffic. Bobbing his head, to the beat of the music. "Baby, can we

stop at CVS." Namira asks, Jahmere. "I need to pick up, my meds."

"Ard, I gotchu." Jahmere says. As his hand, caresses her thigh. He pulls up to the CVS, and double

parks. "Babe, I be right back." He says, hopping out the car. Sprinting into the pharmacy. Namira

decides to change the music. She grabs his iPhone, and puts the code in. Namira begins to search

through Tidal. So, she can find something, that she wants to hear.

As she is scrolling, through the music. Namira hears this voice say. *"But you always going be

my nigga, tho."* Namira, instantly recognizes the voice, she looks up. Va'Shay is standing, right in

front of the car. She imagines herself, getting into the driver side. Starting the engine and running, her

trifling ass over. "Ohh looks who out the hospital." Va'Shay says with a smirk.

Namira gets out the car. "Bitch, I'm getting tired of ya mouth." She says, walking up to her. Not forgetting the fight, they had. Or the fact, that she is the reason, Say'Von is dead.

Jahmere comes out the CVS. "Mira, chill." He says grabbing her. Before her and Shay get into.

"No, let me go Jah!" Namira says. "I'm whoop her ass!" She says, trying to get out of his grip.

"Bitch, you ain't going do, shit." Va'Shay says with attitude. Waving her hand, dismissing Namira altogether.

"Shay, go ahead with the dumb shit." Jahmere says, as a warning to Va'Shay. Trying to hold Namira back, from going off on Va'Shay.

"What the fuck, you going to do!" Va'Shay says to Jahmere.

Jahmere grabs Va'Shay by her throat. "Your fucking days are numbered." He says, squeezing her throat tighter.

"Baby stop!" Namira says, comes up behind him. "You are going kill, that dumb bitch." She says, pulling him off of Va'Shay. "Let her go." People start to crowd around, looking at the drama. That is unfolding, before them. Jahmere lets Va'Shay go, as she grabs at her throat. She stands on the side walk, trying to catch her breath. Not believing, Jahmere just tried to choke her out.

"Get in the car Mira!" Jahmere yells. Walking over, to the driver side and getting in.

"Stupid ass bitch!" Namira says to Va'Shay. As she gets in the car. "When I catch you it's a wrap!"

"Why the fuck, you get out." Jahmere says, snapping on Namira. He pulls into the parking garage, and parks the car. Namira doesn't even wait, for Jahmere to turn off the car. She slams the car door, and walks quickly through the garage. "Don't be slamming my shit!" Jahmere says, getting out the car. "Or, I'm slam ya ass." He says, getting her purse and medicine out the car. They go through the lobby, and get on the elevator. "So, you still mad." He asks with sarcasm. Not wanting to argue, with her anymore.

Namira just ignores him, as they ride the elevator, up to the floor, of their condo. The elevator doors open and she walks off. Jahmere follows behind Namira, and backs her up against the door. She drops her Chanel bag, and puts her arms around his waist. "I can tell somebody missed me." Jahmere says, grabbing on her ass. Namira snatches, the house keys from Jahmere. She opens the door and everyone yells "surprise!" As they walk inside the condo. Jahmere and Namira are shocked, to see all their friends.

"Welcome home sis." Leelee says, giving her a hug. "It's a welcome home/ baby shower." Leelee says, guiding her in the condo.

"I can see that." Namira says, with irritation. "Why the fucking is you here." Her blood is boiling. After the strange premonition, she had in the hospital. Things haven't been right with her. "I want everybody the fuck out my house now!"

"Sis." Leelee says, with a scoff. "You over reacting." She says trying to figure out, why is Namira tripping.

"I don't think I am." Namira says. "Everybody, get the fuck out." Namira says, walking to the front door. All of their friends start to leave, including Leelee and Bahshere. "Ohh no." Namira says. "Lee, you need to stay." She says putting her arm up. "Ohh Bah you too." She says, stopping them from leaving out the door. Namira escorts, the rest of the people out. When the last guest leaves. She closes the door and says. "Now let's get, to the fuck shit."

"Babe, what going on?" Jahmere asks. Not really knowing what is going on.

"Why don't we ask Leelee." Namira says, crossing her arms. "With her, two-faced, lying ass."

"Lied about what." Leelee says, with irritation.

"You never told me the truth." Namira says. Getting straight, to the point. "About what happened, to Say'Von." The room becomes dead silent. Nothing had to be said, it was all on Leelee face. "Listen-" Leelee begins to say, walking over to Namira.

"Ain't no fucking listen!" Namira says yelling. "You and that bitch is sisters!" Namira goes up to Leelee, and slaps her across her face. Jahmere gets up and holds Namira back. "Get off of me Jah!" She turns to Jahmere. "You knew this shit." "Didn't you."

"Baby, wait listen." Jahmere says. "I was booked." He says, trying to get his words together. "I didn't know-" He says, stammering. "We didn't know, one another."

"So, this whole time." Namira says. "My best friend and my fiancé." She says, pacing the floor. "Have been lying to me." She can't even, look at them anymore. Namira is starting to think, that her therapist is right. "Bitch get the fuck out!" Namira yells.

 "Come on Lee." Bahshere gets up off the couch. "Let Mira cool off." He says, ushering Leelee out of Namira condo.

"Yea take her lying ass, outta here!" Namira yells. As the door closes, behind them. Namira turns her attention to Jahmere. "How long did you know, about this." She asks with tears, streaming down her face. Jahmere knew this day would come. He didn't think, it would be today. "All this drama is because of you and Lee." Namira says, walking into their bedroom.

Jahmere follows Namira, into their bedroom. "Baby, listen." "This wasn't how, it was supposed to go." He says. "I didn't know anything about Say'Von." Jahmere explains. "Or him being your brother." He continues to explain. "The thing was, Shay was supposed to make a drop." "Her and her brother." "Now, I don't know why it didn't happen." Namira rolls her eyes. "Instead, she set Say'Von up."

Namira really doesn't care, about the bullshit. She wants to know why. Why, would Jahmere keep something. Like this from her, and not tell her. "Our baby is fighting, for his life." Namira yells. "All because, you and Lee." "Protecting that bitch!" She can't even stand, the sight of Jahmere. Her mind is spinning.

"You acting like, I don't care!" Jahmere replies. "He my son too."

"You better make sure." Namira says, with a smirk. "The other kids yours, too." She says. "Listen I'm done." Grabbing the keys off the table. "I don't care, what you do." Namira says. "Just stay away from me, and my son." Namira takes off the ring and throws it at him. Walking out the door, heading down the steps, to the parking garage. Namira hits the alarm, on the keys. She then realizes, that she took Jahmere keys. She lets out a sigh, and gets in Jahmere's Benz. Speeding out the parking garage, she doesn't know. Where she is going, Namira just drives.

Things are starting to feel like, everything is crumbling around her. Namira bangs her hand, on the steering wheel. Getting off the exist that, is heading towards Penn's Landing. She parks the car, letting out a scream. "How could he, do this to me!" Namira opens up the glove compartment. Grabbing Jahmere glock and putting it, in her purse. She gets out the car, slinging her Chanel purse over her shoulder. Namira starts walking along the pier. She looks up, and says. "Why is this shit happening to me." Her mind begins to race. "First my brother, now my son." She sits on the bench, watching the boats sail on the water. "Mira"! Jahmere yells. Namira turns around, and sees Jahmere and Leelee. Coming toward her, she is really on edge. Namira reaches in Chanel purse, pulling out the glock. "I want the truth, right now!" She yells, getting up from the bench, cocking the gun.

"Mira, just chill, yo." Jahmere says. "We can talk, just put the gun down." He says, trying to calm her down.

"Mira, wait." Leelee says in defeat. "It's all my fault." She says, letting out this long sigh. "It started like this." She begins to tell her, what happened that night:

"Me and Shay never seen eye to eye." "It's always been that way since my parents adopted her." *"Ever since we were teenagers, every nigga I had." "She wanted, or fucked."* Leelee says with venom in her voice. *"So, when Jahmere was doing his bid up State Road." "He left me, Shay and Bah in charge."*

Namira still has the gun pointed at Leelee. "Keep talking bitch, cause if you don't."

"J-j-just relax Mira." Leelee says nervously.

"Don't tell me to fucking relax, now talk!" Namira demands. Firing off a shot, barely missing Jahmere.

"Aye yo, you almost shot me!" Jahmere says, staring wide eyed.

"Yea, next time I won't miss." Namira says, cocking the gun back again. "So, advise Leelee to keep fucking talking."

"So, while Jahmere was booked." Leelee continues to explain. *"Shay started messing, with your brother." "I didn't tell Jahmere, but I advised Shay to chill out." "Cause Jahmere and his crew, was beefing with your brother peoples."*

"So, let me get this straight." Namira says interrupting. "You set me and Jahmere up." She says, with disgust. "Knowing that Shay, killed my brother!" "Bitch you worse than your sister."

"Let me finish." Leelee says, trying to explain. *"Shay was supposed to make the drop." "In exchange, for the kilos of coke." "Me and Bah was supposed to bag the product." "Things didn't go according to plan."*

(December 2016)

Leelee is at her apartment, watching Love & Hip Hop. When her phone starts to ring. "Hello."

"I am in some deep trouble." Va'Shay says. "I need your help." "You gotta come now."

"Shay where the fuck is you!" Leelee says, ready to cuss her out. "You were supposed to meet me and Bah." "So, we could make the drop!"

"I know, I-" Va'Shay says. Faking the desperation, in her voice. "Just come get me please."

"Okay calm down." Leelee says, getting off the couch. "I'm on my way." She says, grabbing her keys. "Where are you?"

"I'm at Say'Von house." Va'Shay says. "On 22nd and Dauphin. She says, before rushing off the phone.

Earlier that day (December 2016)

"Aye zaddy what you doing." Va'Shay says, smiling through the phone.

Say'Von smiles. "Handling some business." He says, counting up the stacks. Putting them through, the money counter.

"I was just wondering if I could come by later." Va'Shay says. "I wanna, sit on that dick." She says, getting straight to the point.

Say'Von can't help but laugh. "Ohh you def can do that." He says licking his lips. "Let me hit you back later."

"Ard baby." Va'Shay says hanging up the phone. She starts laughing at the plan, she is about to execute.

When Leelee parents, made it official. To adopt Va'Shay, on her sixteenth birthday. She felt, she finally had a family, of her own. Va'Shay and Leelee, were thick as thieves growing up. It wasn't till their last year, of high school, at Central. That everything began to change. Namira and Leelee meet, Senior year of high school. The more their friendship developed. The more Va'Shay felt, her and Leelee sisterhood. Was beginning falling apart, well that is the way Va'Shay saw it.

Years later when they graduated high school. Leelee and Va'Shay sisterhood, was no longer. They went about their separate ways. Leelee went on, to college. She graduated from Penn State, at the top of her class. She got her Master's Degree, in Accounting and Business Management.

Va'Shay stayed in the hood. She eventually met Jahmere, and had two kids by him. In the back of her mind. Va'Shay resented Namira, for breaking up their sisterhood. So, when she found out Say'Von, was Namira brother. She came up with the perfect plan. That would hurt, and take something that she loved the most. Her brother.

The Set Up

Va'Shay calls Leelee. "Hey sis." "What time, we meet up for the drop?"

"Later tonight." Leelee says. "Remember meet Ricky, at 22nd and Lombard." She says, rolling her eyes. Praying Va'Shay, doesn't do no dumb shit. "Don't fuck this up Shay."

"Bitch, I'm not." Va'Shay says hangs up. She dials, Say'Von number. "I'm on my way over." She says in a seductive tone.

"The key is in the mail box." Say'Von says. Stacking the kilos of coke, in the duffle. Walking over to his Lexus, and getting in. "I'm see you later." He says hanging up. Va'Shay gets ready, so she can execute her plan. She texts Bahshere, telling him the plan is a go. She goes upstairs to get ready.

About an hour later, Va'Shay hops in her Mercedes coupe. She gets on the expressway, heading over to Say'Von crib. She smiles to herself, as to what is about to unfold. It is like, her evil side is taking over. Every time Va'Shay feels hurt. She feels she must hurt someone, just as bad. Va'Shay pulls up to Say'Von crib, and walks up to the steps.

Va'Shay grabs the keys, out the mailbox. She lets herself in, taking off her shoes. Making herself comfortable, walking around the house. Giving herself a tour. She sees pictures of Namira and Say'Von, together. Various baby pictures and childhood memories.

Va'Shay stops at Namira graduation picture. She picks it up, and says. "Now it's your turn, to feel someone being taken away, from you." She says to the picture. That's when she hears the locks turning. Say'Von comes in, and says "babe you here." He yells, as he comes walking in, through the front door.

Va'Shay puts the picture back, and takes off her clothes. She greets him at the door. Wearing nothing but her bra, and thong. "Hey baby." She says, kissing him on his lips.

Say'Von picks her up, and says. "Damn, you look good." He says, carrying her up to his bed room. Va'Shay lets out a laugh, as he lays her on the bed.

"Come here zaddy." Va'Shay says, unbuckles his pants. Pulling out his already hard dick, and begins to stroke it. She looks up at him. As she puts his dick, in her mouth slowly.

"Ahh shit, that feels good." Say'Von says, grabbing the back of her head. Pushing his dick further, in her mouth. Va'Shay deep throats his dick. She can feel the gagging sensation, but that doesn't stop her. "Aww fuck! Say'Von says. "Turn the fuck around." He orders her. Va'Shay arches her back. Letting Say'Von fuck, her doggy style. He grabs her hair and she let out a moan. "You like this shit don't you." Say'Von says chuckling, and continuing to fuck her roughly.

A few minutes later, Say'Von bust inside of her. They both lay against the sheets, trying to catch their breath. Say'Von goes and takes a shower. While Va'Shay pretends, to be sleep. Soon as the coast, is clear. Va'Shay sends a text to Bahshere. She gets out the bed and calls her brother, Ricky. "Hey bro." Va'Shay says, in a frightening tone.

"Aye yo where the fuck you at!" Ricky voice, booms through the phone. "I'm waiting, and you not here!"

"I got robbed." Va'Shay says fake crying. "I was getting in the car when-" "And, and, they came up and busted my windows!" "They pulled a gun out on me."

"Sis just calm down." Ricky says. "Where the fuck you at?"

"I'm at 1842, near 22 and Dauphin Street." Va'Shay says, fake crying. "It's tha corner house." She says, as she hangs up the phone. Va'Shay creeps to the bathroom door, she can hear the shower still running. Letting her know that Say'Von is still taking a shower. She rushes downstairs and out the

door. Va'Shay smashes her car window out. Making it look like, somebody else did it. Say'Von comes

down stairs and out the door. "Babe you good?" He says, with his gun in her hand.

"Omg!" Va'Shay says, faking like she is upset "Somebody busted my car window out."

"I'm get that jawn fixed." Say'Von says, as they walk back into the house. He goes in the kitchen and

grabs his keys. "Here take the spare to the Lexus." He says handing her the keys.

Shortly after, another round of sex. They hear a banging at the door. "Baby hide." Say'Von says,

getting out the bed. "Don't come out, till I say so." He says grabbing his gun, off the dresser. Say'Von

heads downstairs. Va'Shay hears Say'Von say. "Nigga what the fuck!"

"Where the fuck is the money?" The voice says, waving the gun at Say'Von.

"What money?" Say'Von says, trying to figure out, who these niggas are. They have masks on, but the

voices sound familiar.

"Nigga I'm give you till the count of three." One of the them says. Pointing the gun at his head, as the

red dot dance across Say'Von forehead.

"Nigga fuck you!" Say'Von says. "You going have to shoot me." Va'Shay hear shots being fired. She

can hear footsteps and things being thrown around. Va'Shay throws on her clothes, and climbs out the

window. She has the spear key, to the Lexus in her hand. Va'Shay almost slips off the roof. "Ohh shit."

She says, as she jumps to the ground. Va'Shay falls and bruises her arms in the process.

At the Pier

"So, this whole time you, and Jah knew." Namira says, pointing the gun at them. "And didn't say anything to me."

"I told Lee, not to say anything." Jahmere say. Holding his head down in defeat. "I should have told you, but I didn't want you to think-"

"To think what!" Namira says yelling. "That you and Leelee, been on some bullshit." She says, finishing Jahmere sentence. "Or that, ya'll knew who killed my brother!" "Tell me why I shouldn't kill both of ya'll!" She demands, as the spit, flies out her mouth. "You should have fucking told me." She says.

"Baby, I'm sorry." Jahmere says, walking towards her. Leelee can't move. She never thought, that this would happen.

"Now my son is fighting for his life." Namira says, turning to Leelee. "All because of your sister!" She yells, letting off a shot. Jahmere pushes Leelee out the way. He catches the bullet, in his chest. Namira doesn't even care. Something evil inside of her has been awaken, She is out to get blood.

Leelee rushes over to Jahmere. "Bro it's going to be okay." She pulls out her phone, and she dial 911. Namira walks up to her and aims the gun. "Namira, please." Leelee begs. "Please don't do this."

Namira just keeps the gun aimed, at Leelee forehead. Her mind starts to go blank. She can see the ambulance, and the flashing blue lights. "Bitch, I'm coming for you." Namira says lowering the gun. "I promise you that." She starts walking in the other direction.

Namira hides the gun in her back, covering it with her shirt. Quickly, walking back to Jahmere's car. The tears are streaming, down her face. All she can remember, is her pulling the trigger. She speeds home in Jahmere car. Parking the car, in the parking garage. Her head is spinning, she can't believe. Leelee and Jahmere, would betray her like that. The man that she loved, has been lying to her. And Leelee knew, this whole time. Namira feels, that Dr Benson was right all along.

Namira sees the gun, has fallen to the floor. She picks it up, and open the glove compartment. She sees a large envelop. It says *"DNA Diagnostics Center "* addressed to Jahmere. She opens the envelope, and it reads in bold letters: *"You are 99.9999 percent NOT the father." "Of the above children tested above."* She is shocked, and is relieved.

This is just what she needed. Namira pulls down the mirror, checking herself in the mirror. *"It's going be okay.""* She says to herself. Namira is trying to gather her thoughts. She takes a deep breath, and grabs her Chanel purse. Namira gets out the car, calmly making her way up to her condo.

Chapter 9

On the Way to the Hospital

"You're going to be okay bro." Leelee says, as she climbs in the ambulance.

"Ma'am." The paramedic says. "Can you have a seat, and relax." Leelee sits in the seat. She can't believe, Namira tried to kill her. She can't blame Namira though. It was just a matter of time, before she found out.

The paramedics put an IV in Jahmere arm. "He is stable." One of the paramedics 'yells. As they rush him, to Jefferson Hospital. They pull up, to the emergency room entrance. Rushing Jahmere into the trauma unit. Leelee is right behind them.

The nurse greets them and says to the paramedics. "What do we have here."

"Twenty-eight-year-old black male." "With a gunshot wound to the chest." The other paramedic says "his heart rate is steady." "He is losing a lot of blood."

"Okay, let's get him into the room quick." The nurse says leading him to a room. "Somebody page the doctor now!" She yells. Leelee comes into the room she doesn't know what to do. The nurse comes up to Leelee and asks "excuse me who are you."

"I am his sister." Leelee says trying to get to Jahmere. The nurse stops Leelee from walking any further. "I'm sorry on medical staff are allowed in this room." She says leading her out of the trauma unit, and into the waiting room. "The doctor will be with you when he can." Leelee watches as the doors close behind the nurse. "Shiit!". She calls Bahshere and explains to him what happened.

The doctor comes into the operating room. The nurse attendant, gets him up to speed, as to what has happened. "Okay, I'm going to need 5cc of blood." "Now!" "We are losing him!" The doctor yells to his team. The nurse goes to get the blood to do the blood transfusion. The doctor cuts open Jahmere shirt. He is going in and out of consciousness. They put a sedative in Jahmere's IV. His eyes slowly begin to close. The doctor begins the operation…

In the Waiting room…

Bahshere comes in the hospital. "Aye yo what the fuck happened?!"

"Baby calm down, he's going to be okay." Leelee says trying to calm Bahshere down. The doctor comes out to the waiting room and Leelee rushes up to the doctor. "How is he?"

"Aye yo doc, when can I go see my bro." "Real shit." Bahshere asks trying to remain calm.

"I'm going to need for you guys to calm down." The doctor says. Not liking that he is being bombarded with questions. "I understand the concern but please, calm down."

"Can you tell me how he is doing" Leelee says really worried.

"He is going to pull through" the doctor says, pulling out his x-ray. "The bullet just got lodged into his chest, and as you can see." The doctor says pointing to the X-ray. "It didn't hit any main veins or arteries."

"He had some severe bleeding." The doctor put his hand up, signaling for them to let him finish. "We were able to stabilize him and get the blood transfusions to him just in time."

"Right now, he is heavily sedated." "If you guys want to sit and wait you can." "I have another patient to check up on, and I will back with some updated results a little later" The doctor says leaving.

Bahshere starts drilling Leelee "aye yo what the fuck happened." Leelee tells him what happened. How Namira was trying to shoot her, and Jahmere stepped in the way and he caught the bullet instead. "*He always trying to save somebody.*" Bahshere says to himself. "So, this shit happened because of that trifling sister of yours!"

That's when Leelee mentions how Namira, finds out about Va'Shay setting Say'Von up. Bahshere whole expression changes. "Baby are you okay?" Leelee asks, noticing this weird look on Bahshere face. He isn't paying any attention to Leelee anymore. His minds drifts back to that night.

The Set Up- Plan

Bahshere pulls up on Va'Shay on 17ᵗʰ and Chestnut. She was coming out of the store. A car pulls up and Va'Shay looks. She sees that is Bahshere and she smiles, as she gets in the car. "Hey zaddy" Va'Shay says kissing him on the lips.

See Bahshere and Va'Shay, have been fucking around. Ever since Leelee and Bahshere have been together. With Jahmere being locked up, this the perfect opportunity. Va'Shay knows that is Leelee husband. Honestly, Va'Shay doesn't care. Leelee shouldn't have let her stay with them in the first place *"So wassup with you" Bahshere says giving her the eye.*

"Just did some shopping to clear my head." Va'Shay says. Bahshere can't help but stare. She isn't as pretty Leelee, but she not ugly either. Bahshere weakness is ratchet females. With nice breast and big asses. Which Va'Shay fits that description perfectly.

"What about you, how you been." Va'Shay says licking her lips and rubbing on his dick in his jeans. Bahshere knows what Va'Shay is hinting at.

He merges on the highway. Making their way to Bahshere and Leelee home in East Mt. Airy. "Is she here." Va'Shay asks. As Bahshere pulls up to their driveway and parks the car.

"Stop playing, you think I'm stupid." Bahshere says getting out the car first. Va'Shay rolls her eyes and sucks her teeth. Getting her shopping bags out the back seat. Va'Shay follows Bahshere up to the

front door. He unlocks the door and says. *"To answer your question, she had a business meeting downtown."*

"Ard, cool." Va'Shay says, putting her bags in the foyer. Taking off her shoes. Bahshere know he is violating the code: *"Never sleep with ya Bro "Girl. "Wifey." Or "Side bitch."* Bahshere been wanting to fuck Va'Shay. They messed around here and there. He figured, since Jahmere is booked. This is the perfect opportunity. Bahshere loves Leelee, but Va'Shay is very tempting.

Va'Shay leads Bahshere to the couch, pushing him into the seat. She begins to undress right in front of him, he licks his lips. Bahshere can feel his dick getting hard. Va'Shay starts to do a little dance for him, and he looks with excitement. She twerks her ass, making it jiggle and bounce in his face. Bahshere smacks her on her ass. She looks back and smiles. He pulls her into his lap and he starts kissing on her neck. Va'Shay knows she is wrong for fucking Bahshere. "Fuck it" she thought.

Ever since she laid eyes on him, she had to have him. With his brown chocolate skin, and pearly white straight teeth. His gorgeous dimples in his cheeks, and muscular, tatted up body. Va'Shay thought how could she not fuck him. Va'Shay begins to zip down Bahshere pants, pulling out his dick through his boxers. She strokes his dick until it is rock hard. Bahshere relaxes, and lays his head against the back of the couch. Va'Shay slowly puts his dick in her mouth. Until the entire thing is in her mouth, she can feel herself gagging on his dick.

"Oooh shit" Bahshere says. Grabbing the back of Va'Shay head. Pushing his dick further down her throat. She doesn't lose her concentration.

"Ohh, shit I'm about to cum." Bahshere says loving the sensation.

Va'Shay doesn't stop, she keeps sucking. She can feel the warm liquid, fill in her mouth. Va'Shay pulls his dick out her mouth, slowly smiling as she swallows his kids. Looking Bahshere in his eyes, he is in pure bliss. Bahshere picks her up and carries her upstairs to the bedroom. Bahshere throws her onto the bed. Va'Shay backs up to the top of the bed "come here."

Bahshere takes off the rest of his clothes. Standing in nothing but his boxers. As he makes his way over to Va'Shay. He kisses her on her neck and she pulls his body close to hers. Bahshere caresses her breast. "Damn you fine as shit." He says trying to run game on Va'Shay.

"Nigga please." Va'Shay says, sucking her teeth. "You just in love with this pussy." She says, kissing him on the lips. Va'Shay pulls down his boxers, revealing his hard on dick. She massages it between her legs. Bahshere spreads Va'Shay legs and eases himself in her wetness. She wraps her legs around his waist. As she moans from the pleasure, that he is giving her. "You want to ride daddy dick huh" Bahshere says switching positions.

Va'Shay eases on Bahshere dick slowly. Grinding his inches inside of her. "Now is the perfect time to execute my plan" she thinks to herself.

"Ohh shit baby, I'm about to bust all in your shit" Bahshere says. Va'Shay wraps her arms around his neck. Gently pulling him up closer to her body and continues to grind her waist. Allowing his dick to thrust deeper and deeper inside of her. Bahshere picks Va'Shay up and puts her on top, of the dresser. He thrust into Va'Shay passionately, as she digs her nails into his back. "Who pussy is this" Bahshere demands thrusting into her harder.

"It's yours baby!" Va'Shay moans. "It's yours!" She yells out, in pleasure. Bahshere can feel the nut forming in his dick, and erupting inside of Va'Shay. They both are out of breath. Bahshere goes to take a shower.

Va'Shay is still sitting on top of the dresser, trying to catch her breath. She decides to roll up an L. Va'Shay walks over to the nightstand, and picks up the dutch and weed. She follows Bahshere into the bathroom, and says. "Aren't you and Jah beefing with them niggas up North?" She asks, sealing the L up and lighting it. "Umm, what was the bul name."

Bahshere opens the glass door, turning off the shower. His chocolate six-foot frame dripping with water. Leaving a trail leading down to his semi hard dick. Seeing him all sexy like this, makes Va'Shay pussy wet. She smiles, as she pulls on the L . "You where them niggas be at?" He asks, as he steps out the shower. "Something like that." Va'Shay says with a sly smile. Pulling on the L, as Bahshere grabs the towel. He dries off and takes the L from Va'Shay "explain this info to me, while you suck my dick."

Back to the Present

"Baby are you okay." Leelee says snapping Bahshere out of his own thoughts.

"I'm be back." Bahshere says, kissing Leelee on her cheek. He leaves out the hospital and waits as they valet his car. They bring his car to the front and Bahshere gets in. He gotta make a stop in Overbrook. He hits the expressway, speeding over to Va'Shay house.

Bahshere is doing eighty, on City Line Avenue. In twenty minutes, he arrives at Va'Shay house, barely parking the Benz. He unlocks the front door and yells her name. "Aye, yo Shay!" Going upstairs to her bedroom. He finds Shay sleeping butt ass naked. "Wake the fuck up!"

Va'Shay turns around "nigga why you are yelling." She says sitting up in the bed. Bahshere is so heated, he trying to decided. If he should kill her now. Or just follow through with the plan, that he decided on for himself.

"Hello." Va'Shay says. Getting out the bed and walking in the bathroom, grabbing her Victoria Secret robe.

"I'm ask you this one time, and if you lie to me." Bahshere says. "I'm kill ya hoe ass." He says following her in the bathroom.

"Nigga what the fuck is going on, is it Jah?" Va'Shay asks with concern.

Bahshere grabs her by the back of her neck and ask through clenched teeth. "Did you purposely set up

Namira brother." Squeezing her neck tighter.

"I-I can't breathe." Va'Shay utters. Trying to get his hands off his neck.

"Answer the fucking question!" Bahshere demands, pushing Va'Shay. "I'm not fucking playing with

you Shay!" Bahshere says getting in her face. "Did you fucking know Say'Von was Namira brother!"

"What does that have to do with anything." Va'Shay says not answering his question directly.

Bahshere looks at her with disgust "you a foul ass bitch you know that."

Va'Shay starts laughing. "Nigga you want to talk about foul." "What you think you clean in this

situation." Va'Shay walks over to her bed and sits down. "We been fucking around since Jah been

booked." "Shiit, we still fucking." Va'Shay says laughing. "He going to kill you when he finds out."

"Ohh yea and don't forget about Leelee" she says crossing her arms and sitting on the edge of her bed.

Bahshere really starting to think that Va'Shay is crazy. He gotta figure out something. He hates to

admit it, but Jahmere will kill him. "So, you want to know." Va'Shay says, getting up off the bed and

grabbing the dutch and weed. "Yea I set him up" she says smirking.

Cleaning out the dutch, over the trashcan by the side of her bed. "Had *you* and *Jah* thinking it was them

niggas that ya'll was beefing with." Va'Shay says. Sprinkling the loud in the dutch and sealing it up.

Bahshere temple is throbbing, he smacks the shit out of Va'Shay. Bahshere pulls out his gun, deciding

if he wants to kill her, now or later.

"Do it nigga!" Va'Shay yells, holding the side of her face. She can still feel the stinging of the slap. "If

you that big and bad." She says with a smirk. "I wonder how Lee going to react." Va'Shay says.

"When she finds out, my kids are *actually* yours."

"Bitch stop fucking playing with me." Bahshere says lowering his gun.

"Ain't nobody playing." Va'Shay says going into the bathroom to look at her face.

"It's making sense now." Bahshere says walking into the bathroom. "You jealous of Mira and Lee

friendship."

"Nobody worried about that bitch" Va'Shay says. Noticing Bahshere handprint, on her face. "Look at

my face nigga!" "Fuck."

"You lucky that's the only thing I did to you." Bahshere says as Va'Shay walks out the bathroom,

rolling her eyes at him. Bahshere comes out the bathroom and throws the keys at her. "This shit over

between us." He says walking down the steps and out the house.

"That what he thinks." Va'Shay says watching Bahshere get in his car and pull off. She lay across the

bed. Trying to come up with a plan. It's only a matter of time before Jahmere comes with a vengeance.

Back at the hospital

"The fuck is wrong with Bah." *"He just going leave like that."* Leelee says to herself. Dialing his number again. He picks up on the first ring. Leelee doesn't even let him say anything. "Yo nigga what the fuck was that shit."

"I told you I had some shit to handle." Bahshere says. "I'm almost there, just got off the exit heading to twelfth street now." He says hanging up on her.

Ten minutes later Bahshere comes in the waiting room. He sees the doctor talking to Leelee, she is giving him the death stare. Bahshere ignores her and says to the doctor "how my brother doing."

"We were just about to go and see him." The doctor says leading them to Jahmere room.

"Aye yo bro, how you feeling" Bahshere asks. As him and Jahmere hug. "You trying be a superhero and shit" Bahshere says. They both start laughing and Leelee goes over to hug Jahmere.

"It's ard sis." Jahmere says hugging her. "I'm good."

"Naw all this shit is my fault" Leelee says with tears in her eyes.

"Listen, we made this promise that this wouldn't get out." Jahmere says, taking the blame. "I should have told Mira."

"She is my best friend and I did her foul." Leelee says, feeling the guilt. "I should have never hooked ya'll up." She lets out a sigh. "I hooked you and Mira up, to get back at Shay for sleeping with Bah." Leelee says.

Ever since Jahmere found out, that Bahshere slept with Va'Shay. He has been keeping their relationship, strictly business. "I gotta get the fuck outta this hospital." Jahmere says changing the subject. "I need to see Mira and my son."

"You think that is a smart to do right now bro?" Leelee asks, not thinking that might not be a good idea.

"Aye yo are we going sit here with the sentimental shit." Bahshere says. "Or are we going get back to this money.

"Was you able to meet with the connect?" Jahmere says to Bahshere.

"Yea nigga, that shit is a go." Bahshere says, with excitement. "They going to be coming into the Navy yard, later this week." He says. "They going hit me or you up, with more info."

"Ohh ard, good looking." Jahmere says, resting his head against the pillow.

Chapter 10

(One Month Later)

Namira hasn't been staying at her condo that often. She been too busy with the wedding. Jahmere has been trying to contact her, but she refuses to answer any of his calls. He has been coming to see their son, because Namira checks the visitation log. She goes into the NICU and sees the nurse taking her son vitals. "How is he doing?" she asks, the nurse.

"Hi Ms. Wilson." The nurse says smiling. "Your son is doing much better." "We were able to take the breathing and feeding tube out." She says, checking his vitals. "He is showing signs of drinking and swallowing on his own."

"Good, good" Namira says as she puts her Celine bag in the chair. Walking over to the sink, so she can wash her hands. She dries them off, and goes to pick up her son. "Hey baby boy" she says kissing his chubby cheeks. Namira starts to hum him a little lullaby, as the tears fall onto his little blue blanket. She doesn't even notice that the nurse left. Or Jahmere is coming in. He doesn't say anything, he just watches the interaction between the two of them. Namira looks up, she sees Jahmere standing there. Her whole-body language changes. "What are you doing here."

"I'm here to see my son" Jahmere says, walking over to where Namira is standing. She puts him back in his crib. He starts to whine a little bit, but drifts back to sleep. "Mommy will be back tomorrow" she says kissing his cheek. Making her way towards the door, trying to walk past Jahmere, but he grabs her hand. "Let go of me." Namira says. "Before I slap the shit out of you." She says through clinch teeth, gripping her Celine bag.

"No, we need to talk." Jahmere says in a serious tone, pulling her into his lap. They look at their soon as he is sleeping. "I'm really sorry." He says with sincerity in his voice.

"No, you not." Namira says, wiping the tears away. "I know all I need to know."

Jahmere lets out this sigh. This is the moment that he has dreaded. "Lee told me how Shay set up your brother, and how she took my bread." "All this shit happened, while I was booked." Namira doesn't say anything. His presence and him just being near her. Is making Namira even more furious. "So, when you kept asking me about Shay." "I kept dancing around it and wasn't being straight up with you." Jahmere says. Looking Namira directly, in her eyes.

"I can't trust you Jah!" Namira says, getting off his lap. "You *were* supposed to be the one I could trust with everything." She says walking, back and forth. "You knew how much, my brother meant to me." Namira can feel the anger, rising inside of her.

"What the fuck do you want from me" Jahmere says in defeat and frustration. "I refuse-" that's when Jahmere stops. "Never mind." He says dropping the subject all together.

"You see our son right!" Namira says pointing to the incubator. "You see him!" She is trying to remain calm, but Jahmere is pissing her off. "It's all good tho." Namira says calming down. "I got something for all ya'll asses." She says putting her Celine bag, over her shoulder.

"Can you just calm down." Jahmere says. Honestly, he doesn't even want to argue. He knew that this day would come.

Namira snatches her arm away. "I swear let something happened to my son." She walks out the room and out the hospital. Namira breathes in the March air, and walks over to valet. She hands him her ticket, and waits so they can bring her car. Namira reaches into her bag giving him a twenty. As a tip. She gets in her car and speeds away. Namira is gripping the steering wheel, as she drives over to Overbrook. Namira gets on the highway and she decides to get off at Girard avenue exit. So, she can avoid the traffic.

As Namira is driving, everything is starting to come back to her. The one thing that she can't take, is seeing her son in that condition. She makes her way thorough Parkside. Passing the Mann Music Center. She is ten minutes away from Va'Shay house. The more she thinks about everything.

The madder she gets. Her iPhone is ringing. She looks down and See Jah name flash across the screen. Namira doesn't answer it, she lets it goes to voicemail. She creeps down Va'Shay block, and notices Bahshere Benz sitting outside. "What the fuck his ass doing here." Namira says to herself, notices Bahshere coming out the door. She grabs her phone and starts taking pictures.

"Got his trifling ass and that bitch too." Bahshere gets in his car and speeds off. Namira takes this as her opportunity to run up on her hoe ass. Since she wants to be a dumb ass bitch. She grabs her Celine bag and heads to Va'Shay house. Namira rings the door bell and waits till her hoe ass answer the door.

Va'Shay comes to the door. She doesn't even bother looking through the peephole to see who it is. "Baby you changed your mind-" she says smiling. Her smile disappears when she realizes that Namira is standing in front of her and not Bahshere. "Bitch what the fuck is you doing here."

"I told ya fucking hoe ass, we would see each other right" Namira says. She can feel the adrenaline kicking in.

"Get away from my door." Va'Shay says trying to close the door. Namira pushes the door open, banging Va'Shay in the face. Namira forces herself in. She puts her keys and Celine bag, near the vanity by the window. Stepping out her Jimmy Choo heels.

"So, what you came to my crib to fight me" Va'Shay says holding a bloody nose.

"Yea bitch!" "I'm personally handing you this ass whooping." Namira says squaring up. "Fight me bitch!" She says walking up on Va'Shay, punching her in her face. "Bitch I fucking told you!" Namira doesn't even give her a chance to get up. Va'Shay grabs Namira and pushes her against the wall. They both fall to the floor. Tumbling around on the marble floor. Knocking over vases in the process.

"Bitch get the fuck off me!" Va'Shay yells. Blood is leaking out of her head, blurring her vision. She grabs onto Namira weave.

"Bitch, let go of my fucking hair!" Namira says punching her in the side of her face.

Jahmere comes busting in. He was on his way over to pick up his kids and take them out. "What the fuck is going on!" Jahmere yells not believing what he is seeing. "Namira let her go!"

"Naw, fuck this bitch!" Namira says still punching on Va'Shay. Jahmere is trying to break them apart. He manages to get Namira off of Va'Shay.

"Namira what the fuck is wrong with you, yo." Jahmere says grabbing her. "I come over here to get to the bottom." "Of this bullshit and I see ya car, parked up the street." Va'Shay ignores Jahmere. She charges after Va'Shay, grabbing her by her hair. Namira manages to get out Jahmere grip. Still having her hands wrapped around Va'Shay hair. Dragging her ass back on the floor. "Namira, chill the fuck out!" Jahmere says. Trying to get Namira to let go of Va'Shay's hair.

"She killed my brother and she almost killed my son." Namira says with hurt in her voice.

"You almost killed ya son, trying kill yaself over Jah!" Va'Shay says being a smart ass.

"Bitch! " Namira yells, knocking Jahmere down and slamming Va'Shay head into the marble floor. Punching Va'Shay all in her face. Namira has officially snapped and her anger has taken over. Jahmere gets up off the floor and walks over to Namira, pulling her off of Va'Shay.

Jahmere is trying to get Namira to calm down. "Baby look at me." He has never seen Namira, display this type of behavior. Honestly, it is scaring him. Namira doesn't even say anything to Jahmere. It's like she has zoned out and her mind is somewhere else. She gets out of Jahmere grip and walks over to her Celine bag.

Jahmere looks over at Va'Shay, she isn't moving. It's a pool of blood. Coming out of the back, of her head. He looks up and Namira has the barrel of the gun, pointed in his face. "Baby put the gun down." Jahmere says to her calmly. "Give me the gun Mira." Jahmere says, only inches away from grabbing the gun.

"I will pull the trigger Jah." Namira says aiming the gun at him, and looking over at Va'Shay.

"Baby, I know you hurting." Jahmere says, with pleading eyes. "Don't do this." He says, slowly walking over to Namira. "Now, you care." Namira says laughing. Jahmere grabs the gun, and it goes off. It doesn't hit anybody, but it hits the vase. Shattering it into a million pieces. Jahmere pulls Namira into his arms. She lets out this cry, that has been bottled inside. *"This is what Dr Benson was talking about." "Namira not grieving, properly." "This is just the, beginning…"*

Namira breaks out of Jahmere embrace, grabbing her shoes. She grabs her keys and her purse. Namira

leaves Va'Shay house, quickly. Jahmere is calling after her, but she ignores him. She gets in her car,

and speeds home. Namira attaches the pictures, to a text message. It reads: *"You still want to keep,*

protecting that hoe?" She smiles to herself. Tossing the phone in the seat, as she speeds through City

Ave. Getting off, at the Central Philadelphia exit. She manages to get home, where she hasn't been in a

while. It still feels like home, Namira takes off her Jimmy Choo pumps. And her clothes, right in the

middle of the floor. Walking right in the bathroom, so she can shower. She lets the hot water, hit her

skin. Trying to relax, but her mind is racing.

Namira looks at her hands, and she didn't even realize. How bad her hands are bruised, from

whooping Va'Shay ass. She is wrapped up, in her own thoughts. That she doesn't even hear, Jahmere

come in calling her name. "Namira!" Jahmere yells, through the living room. Storming into the

bathroom. Opening the shower door. Namira jumps a little "shit." "You fucking scared me." She says,

getting out the shower. "I'm the one that Love you Jah." She says, grabbing her robe, and walking in

her bedroom. "Why the fuck you can't see that!"

"I'm tired of this crazy shit." Jahmere says walking away in defeat.

"Nigga you so fucking stupid." Namira yells. "Our fucking son is in the NICU." She says, following

him in the living room. "Let's not forget that shit!"

"I haven't forgotten!" Jahmere says yelling in Namira face. "She still the mother of my kids-" and before Jahmere could finish.

Namira interrupts him "Nigga them bastard ass kids ain't yours!" She says going into the bedroom. Namira comes back into the living room, throwing the paternity papers at him. "Thought I wouldn't find out." "Read it pussy, you are NOT the father!" Jahmere jumps up and grabs Namira by her throat. "Let me go Jah" Namira says with tears streaming down her face.

Jahmere lets Namira go. "I'm the fuck out." He picks up the papers. Sure enough, it says *"NOT the father."* Jahmere needs to get out of there. He already put his hands, on Namira. Jahmere doesn't want it to get worst.

"No, I want to know why!" Namira demands. As her voice starts to crack. "What is with you, and that bitch!"

*"*Move Mira!" Jahmere says, pushing her to the side and leaving.

Namira is trying to process, what is going on. All she wants is for her and Jahmere, to be happy. She figured, Jahmere would be happy to know, the kids aren't his. That they can redirect their focus, on *their* son. Namira meant what she said, she doesn't regret what she did to Va'Shay. She causing too much drama, and problems. Jahmere doesn't answer, Namira's call. He sends her calls straight to voicemail. So, she calls Leelee. She not sure if she going to answer. It has been awhile, since they spoke. She needs her best friend right now. She just hopes she picks up the phone.

Meanwhile in Roxborough

Leelee is steaming mad, about the text she received from Namira. She keeps looking at the pictures.

"This shit is not happening." Leelee says. Not believing what she is seeing. She hears the garage door

opening. Letting her know, that Bahshere is home. She gets out the bed, and waits for him downstairs.

He is unaware of, what he is about to step into. Bahshere unlocks the door, he notices all the lights are

off. Bahshere turns on the light, and sees Leelee sitting in the living room. "Ohh shit, baby you scared

me." He says, walking over to her, trying to give her a kiss. Leelee moves her head, and says. "Why

would you do this to me." Shoving her iPhone, in his face. The picture was clear as day. Him and

Va'Shay, kissing and holding hands.

"B-baby listen to me." Bahshere says stuttering. Leelee smacks Bahshere across the face.

"There is nothing you can say to Bah!" Leelee yells, walking pass him. "Get the fuck out!" She yells

walking upstairs. She now regrets, even taking Bahshere back. He really broke their trust, and she is

officially done.

"Hold up." Bahshere says. Grabbing her arm, before she reaches the top of the steps.

"How long, ya'll been fucking!" Leelee asks. Wanting an answer. Bahshere doesn't answer her

question. "Or, you never stopped." She says crossing her arms. Waiting for Bahshere to reply.

"You a foul ass nigga, you know that." Leelee says. Pushing Bahshere out her way, and going upstairs.

"Maybe this is my karma." Leelee thinks to herself. *"For not telling Mira, what's going on."* She sits

on the floor and starts crying. She can't hold back the tears anymore. Her marriage with Bahshere is

officially over. He comes into their bedroom. She looks up at Bahshere and asks. "Do you love her?"

"Come on Lee." Bahshere says. He really doesn't know, how to answer the question honestly.

"Ain't no fucking come on." Leelee says. Wiping the tears away from her face. "I knew ya ass was still

fucking her."

"Baby, it's not what you think." Bahshere says, still lying and avoiding the truth.

"I'm pregnant." Leelee says sitting on the bed. Not really putting no excitement, behind the

announcement.

Bahshere looks at her with wide eyes. "You pregnant?!"

"Yea nigga." Leelee says, wiping the tears from her eyes. "I'm not keeping it tho."

The vibration from his iPhone interrupts Bahshere thoughts. "Yo wassup bro."

"We need to link asap." Jahmere says. Sitting on the hood of his car, sealing up the backwoods.

"What the fuck happened." Bahshere says.

"Mira crazy ass went the fuck off." Jahmere says, letting out a sigh. "She almost killed Shay." He

says. "I need to go to the hospital and I-"

"I'm go to the hospital." Bahshere volunteers. Grabbing his keys and heading out the door.

Leelee iPhone is ringing, she looks at the caller id. *"Mira"* flash across the screen. She lets it go to

voicemail. Leelee looks through her call log, and find the number she is looking for. She decided that,

what happened in New York. Would stay there, then again what they shared. Ignited an old flame.

Namira's Condo

Jahmere is mad as fuck, most of all the words. *"You are NOT the father."* It is still etched in his brain.

He forgot, all about taking the DNA test. Ever since that argument him and Namira had, back in NYC.

He decided to get the DNA test anyway. Just to prove, that Namira was just going off, as usual.

Jahmere phone is ringing, Namira picture pops up. He doesn't answer, he lets it go to voicemail.

Everything is so fucked up; his son is in the hospital. The kids that he has been there for, are not even

his. Which is what is fucking with him the most. Even though Va'Shay, did Jahmere dirty. He always

tried to look passed that. And trying to be civil, for the sake, that they have kids. Now he doesn't know

what to do. His heart is with Namira, but seeing her wild out. Acting like she crazy, is something that

he can't take.

Namira is blowing up Jahmere phone, but he isn't answering. She decides, to throw on some tights and a shirt. Namira slips on her Fendi slides, and goes to settle the bullshit. She heads down the steps, rushing through the lobby. Letting the crisp air, hit her face and skin. Namira sees Jahmere sitting on the hood of his car. She walks right up to him. "I'm really tired of the bullshit." Namira says. Crossing her arms across her chest, standing in front of him.

"Yo take ya fucking ass in the crib!" Jahmere says. Not wanting to be bothered.

"Naw nigga, we going settle this shit." Namira says. "Right the fuck now!" She says, mushing him in his head.

"I told you about ya fucking hands!" Jahmere says. Getting off the hood, of the car.

"Nigga, I wish you would." Namira says, not backing down.

"Mira go ahead with the dumb shit!" Jahmere says, waving her off.

"I can't fucking win yo!" Namira says yelling. "That bitch doesn't love you!" She says pushing him. "Everything I done is because or for you." "I'm not that bitch Shay!" Namira says yelling in his face. "Never do I sit on my ass and beg." She says, getting upset. "So why can't you love me." "The same way, I Love you."

"Mira, I'm warning you." Jahmere says pulling on the L. Not want to even talk to her.

"Those kids are not yours!" Namira says yelling. "That bitch stole from you." She says, pushing him in his chest. "Yea, I posted up on that hoe." Namira says. "Cause she not going keep disrespecting me." Forcing Jahmere to look at her. "She not going keep doing shit."

"Let, me handle it." Jahmere says, through clenched teeth.

"You ain't handling nothing, obviously." Namira says sarcastically. "So, I did what needed to be done." She says in a serious tone. "She killed my fucking brother!"

Jahmere doesn't say anything. He still upset, about the paternity results. "I knew I shouldn't have fucked with you." He says blowing the smoke in Namira's face.

"So this my fault!" Namira says, not believing what Jahmere just said. "I'm done." She says in defeat. Taking off the ring, sitting it on the top of the hood. "We done and I put that on *my* son." Namira says, walking off. "But you better worry, when I catch Shay, again." She stops and says. "If you stand in my fucking way." "You can catch this shit too." Namira says as a threat. She walks back, through the lobby. Namira is trying to keep it all together, but she can't seem too.

As soon as the elevator doors close, the tears come down her face. It's becoming too much for her to handle. She pulls it together, as the elevator opens to her floor. Namira gets off, the elevator and heads toward her condo door. She walks in, and heads straight to the bedroom. Namira takes off her slides, and gets in the bed.

Chapter 11

Jahmere is still trying to process everything. He picks up the ring, putting it in his pocket. He gets in his car, so he can go and talk to Leelee. About fifteen minutes later, Jahmere arrives at Leelee house. He knocks on the door. Leelee opens the door, to let him in. "Wassup sis." Jahmere says, walking inside the house. Having a seat on the couch, in the living room.

Leelee doesn't say anything, she is trying to figure out. If should tell Jahmere, about Va'Shay and Bahshere. She decides it's just not worth the drama. "Wassup bro."

"Yo good." Jahmere says. Noticing the dried tears, on her face.

"I'm good." Leelee says. Trying to change the subject. "Wassup, with you."

"Yo sis." Jahmere says, with a sigh. "It's a lot of shit going on." He says, shaking his head. "Mira went crazy, she beat Shay up." "She in the hospital, right now."

"Wait, slow down." Leelee says. "What is going on with ya'll?" She asks, getting up. Going into kitchen, pouring her a glass of wine.

"Mann, I don't know." Jahmere says really confused.

Between you and Bah." Leelee says. Coming back, into the living room with her wine. "Ya'll fucking up." She says sitting down on the couch. Having a seat.

"What this nigga do this time." Jahmere says. He finds it strange, Bahshere didn't mention. That him and Leelee are beefing. When they spoke on the phone, earlier.

"I don't wanna talk about it." Leelee says sipping her wine. "You want a drink?" She asks Jahmere, as she heads back into the kitchen.

"Yea, can I get some Henny." Jahmere says. "Namira really wilding." Leelee comes back into the living room with the drinks. She hands Jahmere the glass of Henny. "If I didn't get to Shay house in time." Jahmere says, taking the Henny to the head. "I swear, she be dead."

"Well she deserves that shit." Leelee says, not caring how it sounds. "I'm tired of her trifling ass."

"Fucking shit up between me and." That's when Leelee catches herself, ready to snitch on herself.

"I see what you saying." Jahmere says, taking the last of Henny back. "I don't even, recognize Mira anymore."

"What you mean?" Leelee asks, waiting for Jahmere to clarify.

"Member, how my mom dukes use to act." Jahmere says with a sigh. "She showing the signs." He says. "She already tried to kill herself." "Then she goes and tries to kill Shay."

"I would too shit." Leelee says. "She killed her brother Jah." She says, as if that is a good justification. Leelee phone starts to vibrate. She looks at the caller id. "*Mira*" flashes across the screen. She hits the ignore button. She didn't forget the little stunt. Namira pulled, sending her the pics of Bah and Shay.

"Everything cool sis." Jahmere asks, noticing Leelee attitude changing.

"I'm just tired of the bullshit with Bah." Leelee says.

"I get you sis." Jahmere says. "Peep this fucked up shit." He says. Feeling the effects of the Henny.

"What." Leelee says taking another sip, of her wine.

"So, me and Namira getting into it." Jahmere begins to explain. "She throws some DNA papers in my face."

"DNA papers for what?" Leelee asks, raising her eyebrows.

"Remember that bullshit that happened back in NYC?" Jahmere asks, sucking his teeth. "Well when we got back, I decided to do a DNA test." He pauses before he continues. "And yea, they not mine." Jahmere says, holding his head down. Even him repeating it, makes him upset.

Leelee almost spilled her drink "you fucking lying."

"This whole time, those kids not mine." Jahmere says. Not believing what he is saying.

"So, what you going do." Leelee asks.

"I don't know." Jahmere says. "I'm still trying process this shit." He says putting his head, in his hands.

"I love Mira to death." Jahmere says letting out a sigh. "I just need time, to process this shit."

"I hear you bro." Leelee says. "But, *ya'll* do have a son together." She says to Jahmere. Trying to get him to see, the reality of the situation. "Mira really needs you."

"You right sis." Jahmere says, getting up. "Let me get my ass home then." He says heading to the door. As they say, their goodbyes.

On the drive home Jahmere, has to admit Leelee is right. The more he thinks about it. The guilty he is becoming. Jahmere mind drifts, to how his mother use to act. How mentally unstable she was. That's something that Jahmere couldn't, manage to take. He pulls into their parking garage, and heads up to their condo. He takes a deep breath, before opening the door. Jahmere takes off his Timbs at the door, tossing his keys on the table. He goes into their bedroom. Looking at Namira sleeping, as the moonlight hits her face, and curves. Jahmere licks his lips, making his way over to the bed. Taking his clothes off in the process. Kissing on her neck and caressing her breast, underneath the covers.

Namira turns over "stop it Jah, get off me." She really is not in the mood for Jahmere bullshit.

"I'm sorry, yo." Jahmere says kissing her lips. Not wanting to fight with her anymore. "I am." He says. Slurring his words and gently grabbing her face. She rolls her eyes. "Yea, whatever nigga." Pulling the covers over her and turning back over. Jahmere tries to kiss her, but Namira keeps turning away, from him. That's when he crawls under the covers. Making his way between Namira thighs. He spreads open her legs.

"Jahmere stop." Namira says. As Jahmere turns her over. On her back, pulling her panties off. He buries his head, in between her thighs. Namira lays her head against the pillow. Giving into the tingling sensation and pleasure. Jahmere tongue enters, into her slit. As He slowly, sucks her clit. Pushing his tongue, further and further in her pussy.

"Shit Jah." Namira moans, as she grips the satin sheets, biting on her lip, she can feel an orgasm forming. As her legs are beginning to shake. Namira body begins to levitate off the bed. Jahmere flicks his tongue, against her clit. In short, fast strokes. This sends Namira body in pure ecstasy. "Baby, I'm about to cccum!" She says, as she can feel the orgasm, taking over her body. Jahmere doesn't stop, He continues to suck, and pleasure her pussy. Jahmere can feel her juices, erupting from her. And entering into his mouth. He smiles and continues to drink all her juices up. Slowly making his way up, to her stomach. Kissing on her soft, smooth skin.

Namira reaches in between her legs, playing with Jahmere dick. "Lay back so I can suck it." She says whispering in his ear. Jahmere moves over, to the other side of the bed. Namira smiles, admiring his dick. It smooth and brown, with a lil curve. She grabs it, and begins to stroke it. Slowly putting her mouth, over the head of his dick. Swirling her tongue around the tip. As she bobs her head down, his shaft and messages his balls.

"Damn babe." Jahmere says looking down at Namira. She lets the wetness of her mouth. Drip down the shaft of his dick, and into her hands. You can hear the slurping sounds. Coming from her mouth, as she bobbles her head up and down. "Ohh shit Mira!" Jahmere moans. Watching her suck, the spit off his dick.

Namira looks up at him, and smiles. "Lay back." Pushing him back against the bed. She continues to climb on top of him. Kissing her way up to his face. Namira eases her way, on top of his dick. Letting out a moan of pleasure, coating his dick with her wetness. She rides Jahmere's dick, slow and steady. Jahmere cups her breast licking his lips. "Damn Mira." Namira just smiles and continues, to grind her hips. Jahmere picks her up, walking over to the balcony window. He can feel the effects, of the Henny taking over. Jahmere backs her up against the window, thrusting inside of her. *(To Namira, it is pleasure.)* Taking out his frustrations, on her. All Jahmere can hear, playing over and over in his head. *"You are not the father.* His thoughts are interrupted, by Namira putting her arms around his neck. Kissing him passionately, Jahmere reconnects, with Namira. Caressing his hands, all over Namira's body. "I Love you Jah." She says, looking him directly in his eyes. He carries Namira, back over to the bed.

Keeping himself inside of Namira, laying her on the edge of the bed. He spreads her legs and pins them up. "Ahh shit!" Namira yells. "I'm cumin baby!" Jahmere continues to thrust, inside of Namira. He can feel the nut, rising in his dick. Jahmere just keeps his focus, watching Namira breast bounce. With each thrust, he gives her. I'm cumin too!" Jahmere moans, loudly. As his nut leaves his dick, and into Namira. They both lay on the bed, out of breath.

Namira turns to Jahmere "baby, I'm sorry." She says caressing, his face. "I took it too far." She says, trying to find her words. "I'm sorry, it's just."

"Baby it's okay." Jahmere says. Interrupting Namira, by kissing her on the lips. Namira drifts off to sleep, but Jahmere stays up. His mind is racing, he can't help but think. How Namira has been behaving. It is starting to remind him, of his mother. Jahmere never told Namira how he grew up. A mentally unstable mother, who suffered from a Bipolar Disorder. That is a weakness in Jahmere's life. That he doesn't like to discuss. He watches as Namira peacefully sleeps. The city lights, lighting up the night sky. He gets up, grabbing his phone. Stepping out on the balcony...

Lankenau Medical Hospital

Bahshere is trying to process everything. Including the fact that Leelee is pregnant. It's like his whole world is spinning. On top of everything, Va'Shay is laying in the hospital. Bahshere is speeding to the hospital. He arrives shortly after, hopping out his Benz. Throwing his keys at the valet attendant. Entering through the emergency room. His gold Rolex and chains, shining in hospital lights. He walks up to the receptionist. "I'm here to see a Va'Shay Thompson."

The receptionist is not even paying attention, to Bahshere. She is too busy on the phone. The receptionist hangs up and asks. "What's the last name again?" Bahshere replies impatiently.

"Thompson."

"Damn, you fine." She says, being unprofessional. Bahshere ignores her last comment. He doesn't have time for the games right now.

"We have a Va'Shay Lawson, not Thompson." The receptionist says. Playing in her hair. "Ms. Thompson came out of surgery not too long ago." She says, rolling her eyes. "You can sit right there." She says, pointing to the waiting area. "The doctor will be right out to see you."

The doctor comes out, and the receptionist points over, to Bahshere direction. The doctor heads over, and he holds out his hand. "How is she doing?" Bahshere asks, getting straight to the point.

"Your wife is doing just fine." The doctor responds, noticing the expression on Bahshere face. "Last name *Lawson,* right?" He asks looking at his chart. "Her name is Va." "Vee-Shee."

"It's Va'Shay." Bahshere says correcting him. The doctor's interrupts, Bahshere thoughts. "Yea, where she at." Bahshere says with concern, in his voice. He follows the doctor into the room. He sees her head wrapped in bandages. A tube going through her nose, helping her to breathe. He walks up to her *"damn Namira what did you do."* Bahshere looks at the doctor, and says. "Aye yo doc, is she going to be okay."

"She has suffered some brain swelling." The doctor replies. "Nothing that won't go down on its own." He looks at his chart and says. "I'm afraid there is some bad news." "The baby unfortunately, didn't make it." He says with sympathy, in his voice. "She was about eight weeks." The doctor says, looking at the notes. "We had to do and emergency D&C, considering the circumstances." He says, with sympathy in his voice.

Bahshere can't believe, what he is hearing right now. *"Pregnant?"* He says, to himself. The doctor says, leaving out the room. *"Shit is all fucked up."* He says walking over to Va'Shay, grabbing her hand. Bahshere pulls up a chair, and sits next to her. His iPhone is ringing and he looks at the screen. Jahmere's name flashes across the screen. He takes a deep breath before answering the call.

"Yea, I'm here." Bahshere says. "She going make it, but umm bro." "What the fuck did Namira do?"

"I'm tell you when I see you." Jahmere says. Not wanting to go into detail. About what went down, between Namira and Va'Shay earlier. They hang up, but not before. Jahmere says, he will call him in the morning.

Bahshere holds her hand "baby I'm sorry" he whispers. A tear rolls down his cheek. He wipes it always, before even gets a chance to fall. The doctor comes in "how you are holding up."

"I'm good, doc, but I gotta head on out." Bahshere says getting up, and walking towards the door. "I have some things to take care of."

"Okay, well leave ya information with the receptionist." The doctor says, shaking his hand. "I will keep you updated on everything." Bahshere walks out of the room, heading out of the emergency department. He takes a deep breath, as he walks over to the valet attendant, and hand him his ticket. The attendant tells him, his car will be out shortly. *"I don't believe this fucking bullshit."* His thoughts are interrupted, by the valet pulling up with his car. Bahshere hops in and speeds off, he turns onto City Line, heading home. Then he remembered the fight, him and Leelee had *"shit."* Bahshere decides to check into the Hilton Hotel. Bahshere can't seem to think straight. He decides to make a phone call, but Leelee doesn't answer. So, he leaves a message instead. *"Aye yo Lee, we need to talk."* He says, taking a deep breath. *"I know you mad at me, I fucked up." "Big time, so when you get this hit me up, ard."* Bahshere hangs up, so he can get some sleep. Well at least try to get some rest.

Back In Center City

Jahmere hangs up the phone. He walks back in, and he see Namira standing in the doorway.

"Everything cool?" Namira asks. Walking over to Jahmere, putting her arms around his waist. Resting her head on his back.

"Yea, everything good." Jahmere says. "My bad, I had to call Bah and check up on." Jahmere begins to say. But doesn't finish, he notices the look. On Namira's face. "Nothing, forget it." Jahmere says kissing Namira. Walking back into their bedroom.

"Mmhm, yea ard." Namira says. She doesn't believe it, but not going to press the issue. She closes and locks the sliding door, to the balcony. Jahmere walks over to her, and kisses Namira on the lips. He cups her ass and she smile. "Let's go back to bed baby. " They get in the bed, Namira snuggles up next to Jahmere. She lays her head, on his chest. "Mira, I need to ask you something." Jahmere says, rubbing her back. "Member when you were in the crazy hospital." Jahmere says, trying not to sound rude.

"Yea." Namira says, folding her arms. "Why wassup?" She asks, cutting her eyes at him. "What you trying to say."

"I ain't mean it like that." Jahmere says. Not wanting to upset her. "I'm just worried."

Namira starts laughing, getting out the bed. "Nigga please, you ain't worried about me." She says, with an attitude. "Lately all you been worried about, is Shay."

"Here we go with the bullshit." Jahmere says, with a sigh. He walks away.

"Ain't no *here we go.*" Namira says, mushing Jahmere in his head. "What other proof, do you need." She says, walking to the other side of the room.

"Namira, chill." Jahmere rubs his temple. He can feel, a headache coming on.

"Tell that bitch to chill!" Namira says yelling. Folding her arms, in front of her chest. "She a snake ass Bitch!"

"Namira." Jahmere just wants her, to shut up. Right about now.

"What you mad." Namira says with a scoff. "You thought, that bitch was loyal." She says laughing. "The kids not yours!" She yells. Namira is getting really pissed off. "You want to argue and fight with me." "But show that bitch mercy."

"Mira let it go." Jahmere says, trying to end the argument.

"The fuck you mean." Namira says. "She killed my fucking brother!" She says, walking up to Jahmere.

"The old Jah would have been whooped her ass." Namira says with venom. In her voice. "Or got her stupid ass murked."

"This shit ain't easy for me!" Jahmere says, jumping up in his defense.

"All ties should be the fuck cut!" Namira says, with authority in her voice.

"Yo, go head." Jahmere says, waving her off. He grabs a pillow off the bed, heading back into the living room.

Namira follows Jahmere in the living room and says. "For all we know, the kids could be Bah." She says with sarcasm. "Shit, you just don't want to hear the fucking truth." Jahmere smacks Namira, stopping her from saying another word. A lot is on his plate right now. He doesn't need Namira going off. Getting on his back, about what he needs to do. Jahmere flings her on the couch. "I'm getting tired of ya fucking bullshit."

"Fuck you Jah!" Namira gets up off the couch. Going into the bedroom, slamming the door. She goes in her private bathroom. Namira looks at her face, and her eyes begin to water. She can't believe. Jahmere would actually, put his hands on her. Namira turns off the light, and gets into bed. Namira is at her breaking point. She cries herself to sleep. Letting the silent tears, falls on her pillow.

Chapter 12

The next morning, Namira wakes up with a headache. The events from last night, are replaying in her head. She gets out the bed. Going into the living room, to check and see. If Jahmere is still there. *"Fucking pussy."* She says to herself. Namira goes in her bathroom. So, she can run her shower. She takes her phone with her, checking her voicemail messages. Namira, has a message from her therapist.

"Hi Ms. Wilson this is Doctor Benson." "Calling from Penn Behavioral and Mental Treatment Facility." "It's been a little over two months since I see you." "I wanted to give." Namira decides to save the message. Maybe giving Dr. Benson a call, won't hurt. She gets in the shower, letting the steam relax her nerves. Namira replays *"Baby, I think you need to see ya therapist." "You calling me crazy!" "Naw, it's just."* She finishes up the shower, and turning the water off. Namira grabs a towel. Walking into her walk-in closet, to pick out something to wear for work.

Jahmere comes in from his morning run. The little argument him and Namira had, prevented him from sleeping. He takes off his Nike sneakers. Grabbing a bottle of Fiji water, out the fridge. Jahmere quickly guzzles the water down. He takes a deep breath, as he replays the events in his mind. Especially when he slapped Namira. He heads into their bedroom, and sees Namira getting ready for work. Jahmere watches, as she applies her make up in her vanity mirror. Jahmere walks over to where Namira is sitting. "Can we talk." He asks. Namira doesn't say anything. If looks could kill. "You got some fucking nerve." She says, rolling her eyes.

"Baby, I'm sorry." Jahmere says, cutting Namira off. "I fucked up." Jahmere says grabbing her hand. Namira gets up from the vanity. She continues to get ready for work. Namira checks out, her outfit. In the full-length mirror. She decided on a peachy colored, high waist skirt, and a white blouse. Namira matches her Lou's stilettos, with the skirt to finish up the look. She continues to ignore Jahmere. Taking one final look at herself. Avoiding making eye contact with Jahmere.

"Damn, her ass phat ass shit in that skirt." Jahmere says to himself. Namira tries to walk past Jahmere, but he reaches out. Gently pulling himself, closer to her. Letting her feel his rock-hard dick. *"Damn, he looks good as fuck."* Namira says to herself. Trying not to give in. *"He knows, this makes me weak for him."* *"Bitch, be strong, fuck him."*

"Baby, come on." Jahmere says, trying to kiss her on her lips. "I'm going to be late for work." Namira says turning, her head away. Loosening his grip, from around her waist. She walks out of their bedroom, and into the living room. Grabbing her Hermes bag, and keys.

"So, you just going ignore me." Jahmere says, coming into the living room.

"You said, what you needed to say." Namira says. Cutting the conversation short. "Ard cool."

"We need to talk." Jahmere says in a serious tone.

"I ain't got nothing else to say." Namira says walking to the door. "I'm going be late for work." She says. Rolling her eyes, walking out the door. Namira gets in her car, she decides to call Leelee. She still hasn't talked to her. Since she was being a petty, by sending her those pictures. *"Shit, she needed to know.* Namira thinks to herself. Leelee doesn't answer, she decides to visit her after work. She pulls into the parking lot, and heads up to her office.

"Good morning Ms. Wilson." Her secretary, Ashely says. "Leelee is waiting for you, in your office."

"Thank you." Namira says. "Could you get us some tea please." She says, heading into her office. "Hey sis."

"Ain't no fucking *"hey."* Leelee says, with an attitude. "Bitch!" She says. "How could you do this to me?"

Namira sets her Hermes purse. On her desk "Do what." She replies. Not really seeing, what the issue is.

"You trying to ruin, my life?" Leelee asks. Trying to get to the bottom, of the bullshit.

"What!" Namira says chuckling. "Bitch please." She says, waving Leelee off.

"So wassup." Leelee says. Wanting to know the truth.

"If anybody should be mad." Namira says. Pointing her finger. "It's me." "You supposed to be my fam." She says, crossing her arms. "You knew this whole time!"

"Mira, I'm sorry." Leelee says. "It was a lot of shit going on."

"Still you should have said something" Namira says. She is hurt because, Leelee is more than her best friend. They are basically family.

"I'm just so sorry sis." Leelee says. Walking over to Namira, to give her a hug. Ashely comes in the office, with the tea. She sets it on the coffee table. Namira walks over, to the lounge couch. Leelee sits down, as Namira pours the tea. Handing the cup to Leelee. She takes a sip.

"I'm add a lil *"brown"* to mines." Namira says getting up. Walking over to her desk. Pulling out, the small bottle. "You want some?" She asks Leelee.

"Bitch." Leelee says, rolling her eyes. "It's too early to be drinking."

"Ohh bitch please." Namira says. "It's five 'o'clock, somewhere." She says taking a sip. "Plus, the night me and Jah had." Namira says with a sigh. "I need it."

"I'm pregnant." Leelee finally says.

"Congratulations bitch!" Namira says hugging her.

"I don't think I'm keeping the baby tho." Leelee says to Namira. "Don't give me that look Mira." She says pouring herself, some more tea.

"I just don't know." Leelee says, shrugging her shoulders. "Then you sending me those pictures." She says letting out a sigh. "It's just feels, we need to be for good."

"You going to help me get this bitch." Namira says, with a sly grin. "Or naw."

"Just promise me, no secrets." Leelee says.

"You got some nerve asking *me that*." Namira says in a sarcastic tone. "You knew about Say'Von and his mother." She says, feeling herself, getting emotional. "He was the only family I had left."

Leelee takes a deep breath, before answering. "When I saw you at the hospital that night." She says, with a stutter. "I couldn't bring myself to tell you." "Or maybe you would have thought." She says, shrugging her shoulders. "I had something to do with his murder."

"Well you did a good job, *not* yelling me." Namira says rolling her eyes. "You were supposed to be my fucking family!"

"I was put in an uncomfortable position." Leelee says in a guilty tone.

"So, the fuck what!" Namira says. "You *still* should have said something."

"I didn't know how to sis." Leelee says sadly.

Namira gets up from the couch. She walks over to the window, that is overlooking the city. "Jah always protecting that bitch." She says with her back, still turned to Leelee.

"Ain't nobody protecting her." Leelee says chuckling. "You drunk or something." "Cause now you talking crazy.

"You really think I'm crazy." Namira asks.

"Bitch!" Leelee says. "Ya as crazy as fuck." She says in a joking tone.

"I'm being serious." Namira says, wanting an answer.

"I mean, you have issues." Leelee says. "But bitch who doesn't." She says. Sipping the rest of her tea.

"Wassup forreal." Leelee can sense that there. Is something else, bothering Namira.

"Me and Jah, got in this crazy ass fight last night." Namira finally says.

"Ohh ya'll always going at it." Leelee says. Setting the tea cup on the table.

"No." Namira begins to explain. "That nigga really done lost his fucking mind."

"Bitch, that nigga did what!" Leelee says, getting up walking over to Namira desk. "I will fuck him up."

"Lee chill, let me finish." Namira says, putting her hand up. Before Leelee interrupts, her again. "He is changing Lee, something is off."

"What you mean." Leelee says, sitting on the couch.

"Like for one, I told him them kids not his." Namira says. Leelee doesn't say anything. She just listens, to what Namira is saying. Plus, Jahmere already told her that part. "You think he would be happy." Namira says with irritation. "He started calling me foul."

"Well." Leelee begins, but she stops. "I think, ya'll need to fucking talk." She lets out a sigh. "Jah came over my house." "The night, you fucked up Shay."

"Fuck him." Namira says with bitterness.

"Mira, you gotta chill." Leelee says getting frustrated. "This the shit Jahmere can't take."

"Can't take what!" Namira says getting up. "He not going play me." She says, slamming her fist on the desk. "Our son is still in the fucking hospital!"

"He knows that." Leelee says. "He is worried about you mentally." She says in a calm tone.

"I rather he tells you the rest." She says, walking over to Namira. "I know he loves you sis."

"Does he." Namira says, looking Leelee in her face. As the tears flow from her eyes. "Va'Shay the reason why my brother is dead." She says wiping the tears away. "So yes, I am angry and I'm pissed." Leelee hugs Namira tightly. Namira breaks down and cries. She understands, that she been holding on to this pain. For a very long time. Namira's secretary comes in. "Um, sorry to bother ya'll, but um Jahmere is here to see you." "I told him-"

"You weren't telling me shit." Jahmere says. Walking into Namira office. "I need to talk to you."

"What are you doing here Jah." Namira says, instantly getting pissed off. Leelee decides it's time for her to leave. "Bah wants to meet up." She says rolling her eyes.

"Ard sis call me." Namira says, "Let me know what happens." She says as Leelee is leaving.

"Damn sis, I get no love." Jahmere says as Leelee walks right past him. "I thought we was better than that."

"What are you doing here?" Namira asks, pouring herself some more tea, and adding more Henny.

"It's fucking ten o clock in the morning." Jahmere says. Referring to Namira having liquor, at this hour.

"Okay, I do what the fuck I want!" Namira says, snapping back at him.

"What's up with you yo." Jahmere says walking over to her.

"That's funny." Namira says, chuckling to herself. "You showed me, how you really feel." She says, as her words begin to slur. The sight of being in Jahmere presence, is ticking her off. Namira gets up from the table, and pays Jahmere no mind. He is still talking to her. She grabs her keys, and Hermes purse.

"I'm not finished talking." Jahmere says grabbing her arm. "Where the fuck is you going, yo." Namira snatches her hand away, and leaves out her office.

"I will be back later." Namira says, talking to her secretary. "Okay Ms. Wilson." Ashley says, as she answers the phone.

Chapter 13

Namira grabs her Fendi shade out her purse. She walks off the elevator. Jahmere is watching, as her ass jiggles in her skirt. *"Damn"* he says to himself, as his dick starts to get hard. He goes over to her.

"What do you fucking want!" Namira says. She can feel the effect of the Henny. "Fuck you!" She yells, pushing him out her way. So she can get in the car.

"I'm not moving, till we talk." Jahmere says, with a smirk on his face.

"Talk about what!" Namira says, putting her keys in her bag. "Hmm let's see." "You wanna get mad at me." "For some nutass bullshit, that you can't seem to control." Namira says pushing him in his chest.

"I'm sorry for last night." Jahmere says, embarrassed that he even took it to that level. "I didn't mean to put my hands, on you.

"You think a *sorry* is going to fix everything." Namira says, folding her arms. "Like everything all good right."

"Yo, that not what I'm saying." Jahmere says trying to explain.

"Then what the fuck you are saying." Namira says with hostility. "Cause I'm to a point of *fuck it*!" She says getting her keys out her purse. "You changing, and I hate it."

"Well that makes two of us" Jahmere says under his breath.

"Um excuse me." Namira says, rolling her eyes. "What is that supposed to mean."

"Just fuck it." Jahmere says walking away from Namira. She follows after Jahmere. "Nigga, you brought the shit, the fuck up." Namira says grabbing his arm. "So, explain."

"Naw like you said, fuck it." Jahmere says shrugging his shoulders. "I ain't gotta explain shit to you." He says with sarcasm.

"Nigga, who you think you talking to!" Namira says getting in Jahmere face. "You lost ya mind, you got the right fucking one."

"Back the fuck up." Jahmere says pushing her, out his face.

"Nigga you don't love me." Namira says. "All you care about is yaself."

"Yo, you don't know shit!" Jahmere says. He can feel the anger rising.

"I do know you *ain't shit.*" Namira says. "Our son that is, *actually* yours." Namira says. "He is fighting for his life day in and day out!" She can feel her breaking point coming.

"You not going to understand." Jahmere says letting out a sigh. "Get in the car!" He says snatching her keys, out her hand.

"Fuck no!" Namira says standing there. "Give me my keys."

"Ard." Jahmere says, starting up the Range Rover. "Stay ya stupid ass right there." Namira gets in, cause he ain't going leave her stranded. "Put ya seatbelt on, and enjoy the ride." Jahmere says sarcastically.

Namira just stares at him. Something about his demeanor and aggressiveness, turns her on. A sly smile creeps across her face. Jahmere isn't even paying her any mind. He too busy looking, for music in his phone. He puts on Rick Ross latest album, *"Rather you, than Me."* Letting the music thump through, the surround sound. Namira places her hand in Jahmere lap. Messaging his dick, through his Nike sweatpants. "Aye yo stop." Jahmere says trying to be serious.

"Why." Namira says with a smirk on her face. Namira can't deny that Jahmere, is fine as hell. With his caramel skin. Straight teeth, and gorgeous brown eyes. At times she can't help herself, and these are one of those moments.

"Namira chill." Jahmere says. "I'm trying to drive." Namira ignores what he is saying, and pulls his dick out of his sweatpants. Slowly putting her mouth, over the head of his dick. "Mira, yo you wildin." Jahmere says laughing.

"And you love it." Namira says, as she continues to suck his dick.

"Shit." Jahmere says swerving. "Yo you bouta make me crash."

"Find a spot so I can finish." Namira says sucking on his neck. Sending chills down his spine. Jahmere manages to find a spot, on 22nd and Samson Street. She opens the passenger side of the door. Walking around to the driver side, of the car. Jahmere is watching, with a hunger in his eyes. She stands in front of Jahmere, unbuttoning her blouse. Revealing her black lace bra. walks up to the driver door and opens it. Namira squats down, and pulls his dick out. She pops in her mouth, as it pulsates in her mouth. "Ahh shit Mira." Jahmere says, putting his hand on her head.

Namira can taste his pre cum in her mouth. She doesn't stop sucking. Namira can feel the nut forming, in the top of his dick. Jahmere shoves his dick in her mouth, as the cum flows out his dick. She swallows his cum and continues to suck Jahmere's dick. Giving Jahmere a crazy sensation, that he can't seem to handle. She gets in the back seat "come here zaddy." Namira says pulling him in the backseat with her. Climbing on top of her, kissing on her breast and unhooking her bra. Namira lets out this moan of satisfaction. Jahmere sucks on her nipples, and she grabs his head kissing his lips passionately. Jahmere lifts her skirt and Namira pulls Jahmere dick, out his sweatpants. He pushes Namira thong to the side, entering inside of her. Namira smiles, pulling Jahmere closer to her body. As her skirt rolls up to her waist. "Ooh shit Jah." Namira says moaning. "I Love you Jah."

"You love me." Jahmere asks, thrusting even deeper. Inside of her. Namira pushes herself on top of Jahmere. Pushing him against the backseat, of the car. The windows are starting to fog up. From the body heat, that they are creating. He moves Namira hair, out of her face. "Mira, I Love you." He says looking into her eyes.

Namira kisses Jahmere. "I Love you too Jah." She says bouncing on his dick. She can feel the orgasm

forming, in her body. As she clutches, onto his body. Jahmere just smiles, he can feel the wetness,

coating his dick. Namira allows the orgasm to take over. As she cums all, over Jahmere dick. She falls

into Jahmere's arms. Coming down, from the euphoria of the orgasm.

"Namira." Jahmere says, as Namira lays on his chest.

"Yes baby." Namira says looking up at him.

"You know I love you." Jahmere says caressing, Namira's chin. She doesn't say anything. Namira just

enjoys the moment. "Namira did you hear me." Jahmere says, interrupting her thoughts.

"Can we just enjoy the moment." Namira says with a sigh. Sitting up, rolling her eyes. Getting off

Jahmere lap, buttoning up her blouse. "Here we go." Jahmere says, noticing Namira's attitude.

"Nigga, whatever." Namira says, getting out the backseat. So, she can fix her skirt. Making sure

nobody is around, as she fixes her clothes. Jahmere gets out and fixes his sweatpants. Walking back

over, to the driver side of the car. Namira is fixing her hair and touching up, her make up. Jahmere just

keep staring at her. Namira can feel his eyes. "So where are we going?" She asks, looking over at

Jahmere.

"Don't worry about it." Jahmere says, with a sly smile. He starts the Range Rover. "Just enjoy, our

quality time."

Lankenau Hospital

"How is she doing?" Bahshere asks the doctor. As he comes into the room.

"We want to keep her, for a few days." The doctor says, looking over Va'Shay chart. "She suffered some brain hemorrhaging." The doctor sees the look, on Bahshere face. "We want to make sure the fluid, is no longer present." He says, easing Bahshere's mind. "She does have some swelling as well." "Due to the force and the damage to the brain." The doctor says. "She might experience, temporary memory loss."

Bahshere iPhone is ringing, interrupting the doctor. It's a face time from Leelee. He almost forgot, that they meeting up. Bahshere needs to come clean, about some things. "Ard well doc, I have to handle a situation." He says texting Leelee, telling her he is on his way. "I will be back tomorrow morning." Bahshere says, as he heads out the hospital. His phone starts ringing again. He answers with a "yo."

"Don't yo me nigga." Leelee says, yelling through the phone.

"Aye yo chill the fuck." Bahshere says. "I'm on my way to meet you." He says matching Leelee attitude.

"Whatever nigga." Leelee says. Hanging up the phone, in his ear. Bahshere lets out a sigh, everything is so fucked up. He still loves Leelee, but their marriage, has ran its course. It doesn't help, he has been sleeping with Va'Shay. Ever Since their marriage began.

Bahshere pulls into, the Chill's on City Line Avenue. He sees Leelee, she is leaning against her Benz. Waiting with her Versace glasses on. He parks next to her and gets out. Bahshere has to admit she looks good as ever. Tight fitted crop top. Showing her perky breast, and distressed denim jeans. Her Giuseppe stiletto heels, and her Halle Berry haircut, completing the look. His dick gets hard, just looking at her. He starting to regret even telling her about him and Va'Shay.

"You said you wanted to talk." Leelee says. "So, start fucking talking." She says, not wasting any time. "Cause last time we spoke." "I was about to kill ya ass." Leelee says. Not giving Bahshere, a chance to speak. "How long, ya'll been fucking."

"Leelee, let me explain." Bahshere says, trying to get a chance to speak.

"Explain what nigga!" Leelee says, raising her voice. "You been fucking around with this bitch!" She says, walking up on Bahshere. "You creeping out late at night." Leelee continues to say. "Lying saying you and Jah, gotta handle business." She says getting in his face. "You were fucking her!"

"Nigga, you lucky we in public." Leelee says. She really wants to get her gun. "So, she was telling the truth." Leelee says with a scoff, punching him in his face.

"The fuck, Lee!" Bahshere says, holding his bloody nose.

"Fuck you nigga!" Leelee says, ready to go off on him. Bahshere is checking his lip. He can feel the blood, spilling in his mouth. "I fucked up."

"I been there since day one!" Leelee says. "Nigga I'm the one moving ya money!" "Making sure that shit legit." "We been together since we were teenagers." She says, as her voice begins to crack. "You want to throw away, away just like."

"Baby." "I-" Bahshere says, trying to explain.

"People was telling me." Leelee says. "I didn't want to listen." She says shaking her head. "Answer this question, is the kids yours?" "Since they not Jah?" Bahshere has this dumb look, on his face. "Yea, DNA don't lie." Leelee says. Folding her arms across her chest. "Jah ain't the father, so that just leave you." She says pointing her fingers at him. "Wait till Jah find this shit out." Leelee says, laughing. "Ya ass going be six feet under."

There is nothing Bahshere can say, to justify the situation. He fucked up, and he has to face, the consequences. Jahmere is going to kill him. When he finds all this out. Bahshere is going to have to find a way, to tell Jahmere. The setting Say'Von part up. He didn't know, that was Namira brother. Had he known. Bahshere wouldn't agree to the plan. All because his greed, and the power of pussy. It's about to cost him everything.

Leelee takes off her marriage ring "this use to mean, so much to me." She says throwing the ring at him. "She can have you." Leelee says. "I'm have them papers printed up." She says walking off. "I'm let you know when to sign them." She can feel the tears, forming in her eyes. Leelee refuses to let

Bahshere, get the best of her. He not even worth her shedding any tears. Leelee knew their marriage, was over. She didn't expect it, to end like this.

"What about the baby." Bahshere asks, wanting to know.

"Nigga, what baby." Leelee says walking away. She hops in her Benz and speeds off. Letting the tears flow from her face. She is heartbroken. Leelee built her life, with Bahshere. They we're high school sweethearts. Then she graduated from college, and started helping Bahshere. Moving the money, and investing it into the stock market. Leelee grabs her iPhone and makes a call. A sexy voice answers.

"Yo ma, wassup" the voice says. That New York accent, gets her every time.

"You still in Philly." Leelee says. "Or naw?" She asks, smiling through the phone.

"Yea, my flight doesn't leave till tomorrow." The voice says. "I'm staying at the Ritz Carlton, downtown suite 236." "I'm leave the key, at the front desk." He says, as hang up.

Leelee merges on the expressway. Driving towards the Ben Franklin/Avenue of the Arts, exit. She is weaving in and out, of the down traffic. Reaching the Avenue of the Arts, trying to find a parking spot.

After about twenty minutes, of fighting traffic. Leelee finds a parking spot. She puts money in the kiosk, and puts the ticket in the front of her window shield. Leelee puts her Chanel bag, over her shoulder. She walks about two blocks, to the Ritz Carlton. Leelee walks into the lobby, up to the receptionist. "Hi, good afternoon." "I'm here to see a Mr. Lawson."

"Ah yes, let me double check." The receptionist says, typing on the computer. Her iPhone starts ringing, she looks down, it's *Bahshere*. Leelee sends the call to voicemail.

"Everything is correct, here is your key." The receptionist hands, the key card to her. "The room is 236." "The elevator doors, are straight ahead."

"Thank you." Leelee says taking the keycard.

"No problem." The receptionist says, with a smile. "Enjoy your stay at Ritz Carlton."

Leelee heads to the elevators. Preparing herself for the encounter, she is nervous. She checks herself, in the elevator reflection. Making sure she still looks fly, and she does. The elevator stops on the floor, and Leelee gets off. She walks up to the room, and uses the key card. Letting herself in. "Baby you here." She says, putting her Chanel bag in the chair. She sees a trail of roses, leading to a table set for two. "Quinel, stop playing."

That when a pair of strong arms, grip her waist. "A little surprise, for my baby." He says in a sexy New York accent. *"See Quinel is Jahmere's blood brother, and Jazmine's husband, but that's according to her. Quinel says, they are no longer together."*

Before Leelee, met Bahshere. Leelee and Quinel dated back, in high school. They parted ways, when she found out. He was fucking with Jazmine. Namira's *"best friend."* Leelee ended the relationship, and started fucking with Bahshere. She rekindled the old flame, when she and Namira was in New

York. Ever since then, Quinel has been calling nonstop. He even sent Leelee gifts, and even made a couple trips to her job. She would always blow him off. Or act like, she was too busy. "You know I miss you." Quinel says, pulling her into a warm embrace.

Leelee rolls her eyes, and gets out of his embrace. She walks over to the food "what's this." She says lifting the silver cover, off the plates. Revealing a delicious lobster entrée. "Aww you remember."

"How could I forget." Quinel says walking over to her. "How I let you slip away, from me ma." Quinel asks. Invading Leelee's personal space.

"You know what, let me go about my business." Leelee says, getting out Quinel grip. "This was a mistake, that I'm even here." She says grabbing her Chanel bag, putting it over her shoulder.

"Wait, wait ma." Quinel says blocking the door.

"Move Quinel." Leelee says. Not wanting to deal, with his shit either.

"Naw, Ma." Quinel says walking up to her. As his 6'6 frame towers over her. Leelee can smell the YSL cologne. *"Damn, this nigga smells good as shit."* She says to herself.

"The least you can do, is sit and eat with me." Quinel says grabbing her hand. Leading her to the table, and pulling out her chair. Trying to charm her into staying. Leelee puts her purse on the table, and takes a seat.

"So, what is new with you Quin." Leelee says changing the subject. Enjoying the delicious meal.

"Well, I'm glad you asked." Quinel says. With this goofy grin, on his face. "I might be moving back to Philly." He says, taking a bite of the entrée. "You spoke to Jah." Leelee says with an irritation.

"Chill ma." Quinel says. "I ain't say shit about us." He says with reassurance.

"Oh ard." Leelee says. "Cause I gotta tell, Mira." She says, taking a bite of lobster.

"The fuck you her for." Quinel says with an attitude.

"We tell each other everything." "Since she so *cool* with that hoe." "I mean Bitch." Leelee says. "My bad *Jaz.*"

"I want to show you something." Quinel says. Stuffing some more lobster, and rice in his mouth. Getting up from the table, and walking over to the chair. Where his Burberry duffle is sitting. He opens up the duffle bag, and pulls out an envelope. Leelee doesn't say anything, she continues to eat her food. *"I know this nigga don't think, we together or some shit."* Leelee says to herself. Quinel interrupts Leelee's thoughts, by saying. "My divorce papers." He says, handing the envelope to her. Leelee almost chokes on her food. She gets up from the table. Walking over to the couch to take a seat.

Quinel pours two flute glasses of Moet. He hands one to her. "I Love you *Lee*, always have." A tear rolls down her face. "Ma what's wrong." Leelee is silent, she can't seem to keep it together. She dreaded the fact that this would happen.

She never got over Quinel. It was more of a buried hurt. That she decided to keep, locked away. Not to say that she didn't love Bah. It was something, she had to learn to do. It didn't come naturally, as it did with Quinel. "Lee talk to me" Quinel says.

Leelee ignores him and walks toward the window. She been wanting to ask this question. Since they broke up, almost fifteen years ago. Leelee lets out a sigh "why her."

"What you talking about yo." Quinel says, walking over to her.

"You heard me." Leelee says turning around. "Why did you fuck her."

"Ma come on we was fucking teenagers." Quinel says. "My stupid ass didn't know any better." He says holding her, in his arms.

"So, what." Leelee says. "I gave you my virginity." She says with hurt in her eyes. Pushing him away, not wanting to argue with him.

"I was young." Quinel says with agitation. "She wasn't nothing to me, yo."

"You married the fucking bitch!" Leelee says. Taking back the Moet, and pouring her another.

"Yea I did." Quinel says. "You wasted no time." "Marring that bum ass nigga, either." He says, referring to Bahshere.

"That was *after* what you did!" Leelee says, pointing her finger in his face.

"My nigga, is *you* serious right now." Quinel says, in his New York accent. "Why we arguing about irrelevant shit."

"I'm not supposed to be here." Leelee says, shrugging her shoulders. Drinking the rest of the champagne, in her glass.

"Yea ard." Quinel says taking off his shirt. Walking over to her. Leelee can't help but to stare. "S*hit.*" She says under her breath. Leelee knew this would happen, if they meet up again. Quinel walks over to where Leelee is standing. "Damn you look good." He says, licking his lips. "Got ya hair all done and shit."

"Stop Quin." Leelee says pushing him away, but really wanting to fuck the daylights out of her.

"Make me." Quinel says. Picking her up, and carrying her to the master suite. Gently, tossing her body on the bed. Leelee can see his dick getting hard. It is making her pussy wet. He lifts her shirt, up and off her head. Letting her breast be exposed to him. Her boobs are not big, but they aren't small either. Just the right size, for him to grab and suck. "Damn." Quinel says kissing on her neck.

"We gotta stop." Leelee says, sitting up on the bed, trying to pushing him off of her.

"Why." Quinel says unbuttoning his jeans. Letting them fall to the floor. He pulls down his boxers and says. "You know you missed this ma." He says, sucking his teeth. "Stop frontin."

Quinel continues to kiss on Leelee body, as she lays on the plush sheets. He pulls down her jeans, revealing her red thong. Kissing on her pussy, he can taste her juices. That are already soaking, between her thighs.

"Baby stop." Leelee says. Looking at him, licking between her thighs. He buries his head, deeper in between her legs. Moving her thong to the side. Sucking on her clit, inserting his tongue in her pussy. Making her legs buckle "Quin, baby stop." Leelee moans with pleasure. Quinel's tongue, enters inside of her pussy. She can't seem to silent the moans, that are escaping from her mouth.

Quinel looks up at her, and asks. "You're sure you want." He says looking Leelee directly, in her eyes. "Me too." Quinel says, finger fucking her pussy. "Lay that pretty ass back." He says, helping Leelee out her jeans.

"Baby, let me take off my shoes." Leelee says, sitting up in the bed.

"Naw ma." Quinel says. "Leave them on." He says, pushing her back down on the bed. Quinel gets on his knees, and pulls her legs to the edge of the bed. Slowly, sucking on her pussy lips. Letting her legs rest on his shoulders.

"Damn Quin." Leelee moans, pushing his head, further between her thighs. "That feels so good, baby." She moans, out with pleasure. Quinel slowly licks up, and down on her clit. Sending her body, into an ecstatic shock. "Damn, ya shit wet." He says, sucking the juices. That are spilling all over his lips, and fingers. Quinel leaves the bedroom, grabbing the bucket of ice. Putting a few pieces in his mouth, walking back into the bedroom.

"Baby, why you leave?" Leelee asks, sitting up on her elbows. Quinel ignores Leelee. Placing the ice

bucket, on the nightstand. He walks over to the bed. Lifting her legs back up, and placing them back on

his shoulder. He slowly inserts the ice, into Leelee's pussy.

"Quin." Leelee begins to say." Feeling the effects of the ice. Giving her a cold feeling, mixing with her

juices. Quinel slurp it up, as it falls into his mouth. Flicking his tongue, in fast strokes against her clit.

"Baby I'm about to cum!" She moans, feeling the orgasm building up, and explode from her body.

"Ohh shiit Quin!" Leelee yells out. "Baby, I'm cumin!" She says, as her body levitates off the bed.

Leelee can feel herself cumin in Quinel's mouth. He smiles as he watches Leelee's body, shake and

twitch.

Quinel climbs on top of her kissing on her stomach. Making his way, up to her lips "Lee, I love you."

He says, looking her in her eyes.

"I Love you too Quin." Leelee says smiling. Quinel spreads her legs open, inserting himself, slowly.

"Yess!" Leelee says, biting on her bottom lip. Keeping herself from screaming out, in pleasure. She

wraps her legs, around Quinel's waist. He backs her up against the wall, fucking her even harder. This,

turns Leelee on even more, as she bites his lower lip.

Quinel turns Leelee around, bending her over. Leelee grabs her ankles, and starts twerking her ass.

"Yea bounce that shit!" He says, as he grabs her by her waist. He is fucking her so good, that her legs

begin to get weak. "Naw ma, don't fall." Quinel says, taking his dick out. Grabbing her arms, putting

them behind her back.

Quinel guides Leelee, over to the table. It is sitting in the middle of the room. He bends her over slowly, stroking her pussy.

"Ohh zaddy yess!" Leelee moans out, as her pussy begins to get wetter. "Harder baby!"

"Shut up!" Quinel says, forcing her to lay flat on the table. "I swear ya shit the best." He grips her waist even tighter. "Arch that shit a little more ma." Quinel says, deep dicking her pussy from the back. He can feel the nut forming in his dick. He pulls out, busting all on her back. "That felt good." Quinel says smacking her on her ass, and heading to the shower.

Leelee is still trying to catch her breath. *"Damn, his dick good as shit"* she says to herself. She sees the weed, and the dutch. Laying on the night stand, she might as well spark up. Leelee is cleaning the guts out the dutch. When Quinel phone begins to ring, her curiosity is getting the best of her. Leelee starts to walk over, to answer Quinel's phone, but then she stops. *"What am I doing."* She says to herself. *"He not my fucking nigga."*

Quinel yells, from the bathroom. "Aye yo ma, come get in the shower with me!"

"Here I come baby!" Leelee yells back. Putting the dutch, and the weed back on the table. She goes into the bathroom, she stops at the door. Leelee admires Quinel, through the glass shower. With his, caramel skinned complexion. Sexy chiseled body, and Caesar waves poppin. Just her reflecting on it, makes her pussy wet, all over again.

Chapter 14

Quinel opens the shower door "come join me." He says, as Leelee takes off her Giuseppe shoes.

Carefully, getting in the shower. Letting the steam hit her face. She lets the hot water hit her back.

Washing off Quinel's cum, and getting her hair wet. "You paying to get my hair redone." Leelee says,

turning around facing Quinel.

"That ain't nothing." Quinel says, backing her up against the shower door. Leelee pushes Quinel

against the wall. Kissing on his tattoos, making her way down to his dick. She grabs it, and slowly

begins stroking it. Quinel body, relaxes against the wall of the shower. Leelee puts his dick in her

mouth. Letting it slide down her throat, and messaging his balls simultaneously. "Shit." He says,

pumping his dick, in and out of Leelee's mouth.

"I need to hit that again." Quinel says, pushing Leelee up against the wall, and fucking her. He grabs

Leelee legs, and she wraps them around his waist. Quinel continues to give Leelee. Long, deep strokes.

"Mmm, yess baby." Leelee moans. "Don't stop, baby don't stop." She says, kissing on his neck, as the

water runs against their bodies.

"Fuck!" Quinel whispers, pinning her against the shower, and nutting inside of her. They both, are

trying to catch their breath. As, the water begins to turn cold. Quinel is the first one, to get out the

shower. He grabs the robe, and heads into the bedroom. Leelee finishes washing up, and steps out the

shower. Grabbing a towel, and heading in the bedroom as well. She finds Quinel, rolling the L up and

sparking it.

"Damn." Quinel says, as he watches Leelee walk across the room. Getting her phone out her Chanel

purse. "Baby look in my duffle" he says, pulling on the L.

Leelee is checking her phone. She notices that she has two missed calls from Bah. She goes to his

contact and deletes his contact.

"Why what's in there." She says redirecting her attention to Quinel.

"I think you going like it." Quinel says with a smile. Leelee rolls her eyes, and looks in the duffle bag.

She finds a black velvet box, with a satin ribbon on the top. "Baby, what's this?"

"Open it ma." Quinel says. Getting out the bed, and walking over to her.

Leelee opens it "oh my God." She says. "Baby this is beautiful!" Taking out the, twenty-four-caret

heart pendant. Embellished in white diamonds.

Quinel puts his L out, in the ash tray. "Let me help you put it on." "This is beautiful baby." Leelee

says, admiring the necklace. "Yea, look at the back." Quinel says, turning the pendent over. In cursive

letters it reads: *"Q&L forevah."* He puts the necklace, around Leelee's neck. "You always have my

heart ma." Quinel says, kissing on her neck. "I let you go the first time." Kissing her on the lips. "I'm

not letting you go again." Leelee grabs his hand, and leads him over to the bed. Quinel kisses her lips

and untying her robe, as she lays back against the pillows. Quinel kisses on her breast, sucking on her

areola. Sending a tingling sensation, throughout Leelee's body. He runs his tongue, down her

midsection. of Leelee body. Quinel buries his head, in between Leelee legs, sending Leelee into pure

bliss.

In the car

"So, baby where are we going?" Namira asks as they get on the expressway. Heading towards City Line Avenue.

"Can you chill out" Jahmere says weaving, in and out of the traffic. Getting off the exit for City Line Avenue.

"Why are we here." Namira says with excitement. "You taking me to Saks, so I can get that new Fendi bag."

"Naw" Jahmere says laughing. "We having lunch." He says, with a smirk. Namira frowns her face and says. "Babe, I gotta get back to work."

Jahmere pulls into the parking lot. Of the City Ave shopping center, and says. "I told Ashely to cancel ya meeting for today."

"What!" Namira says unbuckling her seat belt and getting out the car. "Babe that's money I'm losing."

"Yo calm down." Jahmere says getting out. "You already know I gotchu." He says hitting the car alarm. "Chill" he says kissing Namira on the lips.

"Okay" Namira says putting her Hermes bag over her shoulder. They walk up to *"Wing Stop"* and she has this confused look, on her face. "Why are we here" she asks.

"Remember when we had our unofficial/ first date in Atlanta at the Wing Stop." Jahmere says, jogging Namira memory. "Ohh yea, I remember."

It was when Leelee and Namira, went down to Atlanta. So Leelee could visit her family, and the same

day she met Jahmere. Leelee mentioned Jahmere to Namira, hoping that they would hook up. Namira

heard about Jahmere. From what she knew, he had somebody, but word around Philly, they were no

longer together. When Leelee asked her if she wanted to go to Atlanta. Namira figured *"fuck yea,*

bitchhhhh its Atlanta." Both of them meet up with Bahshere and Jahmere, at the Wing Stop to grab a

bite to eat.

When Jahmere saw Namira he couldn't help himself. It could have been the fact, he ain't have

pussy in over a year. Or she was just fine as shit, and he thought both. So Jahmere asked Leelee about

who Namira was and Leelee told him. That Namira was single. and the rest is history. Namira begins to

smile. "Yea, that was a good day." She says laughing. "I got barbecue sauce on my shirt."

"Yea, and you basically ran out the restaurant." Jahmere says laughing. "I also remember how juicy ya

ass looked in them cut up shorts too."

"Ohh whatever nigga." Namira says playfully hitting him in his arm. Jahmere opens up the door, letting

Namira walk in first. They walk up to the counter and order their wings. Namira orders the Lemon

Pepper, and Jahmere gets the Garlic Parmesan. They get their food and have a seat by the window.

"Babe, these jawns good." Namira says wasting no time eating.

"I know right." Jahmere says enjoying the wings as well. "We need to talk." He says, in a serious tone.

Namira attitude switches up. "See I knew this was some bullshit."

"Evelyn shut up!" Jahmere says in an outburst. His temple is starting to throb, this is what he didn't want to happen.

"Who the fuck is Evelyn." Namira says, rolling her neck and crossing her arms. People are starting to stare at them. Namira gets up and Jahmere grabs her arm. "Namira, please sit down." He says pushing her in her seat. "Who is Evelyn Jah." Namira asks, demanding an answer.

Jahmere takes a deep breath "Evelyn is my mother." He says taking a deep breath. "This is what I wanted to talk to you about." He begins to tell him about his childhood: *"Me and Quinel grew up in North Philly." "We lived with our mother in a two-bedroom apartment on Ridge and Girard Ave."* "Go ahead I'm listening." Namira says holding his hand.

"It was just us, no dad around. That nigga was in and out our lives constantly." "My mother would take him back every time." "I guess because she loved him." He says, taking another bite of a piece of chicken. *"That what she would tell me when I asked her."*

"See my dad was this big-time drug dealer in North Philly." "I'm talking major keys." "I guess the apple didn't fall too far from the tree, being as though how me and my bro turned out." He says chuckling to himself, to keep the tears from falling. *"I never understood why mom never moved us out the hood.". " Anyway, her and my dad was having this big ass argument, I don't remember how old we were, but umm this nigga just left." "Like he just never came back." "I felt that his hustle was more important than us, or my mother, and he choose tha streets."*

Namira has never seen Jahmere so vulnerable and open like this. You can hear the hurt as he spoke. *"That broke mom dukes' man, like it broke her to a point that was internal, like a never healing wound, and that-"* Jahmere begins to choke up. This the first time that he has really opened up to someone, about his mother. *"I have watched my mom lose her mind."*

"What, you mean loose her mind." Namira asks interrupting Jahmere. He looks Namira straight in her eyes. "My mom was diagnosed with Bipolar disorder-"

"What does that have to do with me!" Namira says cutting Jahmere off.

"Mira, I think you should see ya therapist, again." Jahmere says, really concerned about her mental health.

"So, what you saying I'm crazy." Namira says not liking, what Jahmere is hinting at.

"No, but I can't take losing somebody I Love and care about." Jahmere says holding Namira hand.

 "When you fucked up Shay, you been different." "I saw that look in ya eye when you had that gun."

Namira snatches her hand away. "Just cause ya crazy ass mom lost her mind." Jahmere excuses himself and says "let me leave before I fuck ya dumb ass the fuck up." He says storming out of the restaurant.

"Jah, wait baby hold on." Namira getting up from the table. Following right behind Jahmere. She sees him outside leaning against the Benz, smoking an L. "Its good." He says getting in the car.

Namira hops in, letting her purse fall to the floor. "I'm sorry."

Jahmere just looks at her, and it reminds him, so much of his mother. He starts up the car, he doesn't

know if he should be hurt or understanding. Jahmere grips the steering wheel, as his thoughts consume

him. Namira notices his body language. *"Shit maybe he is right."* She says, reflecting on what

Jahmere was saying to her. Namira starts rubbing on Jahmere's crotch, putting her hand in his pants.

The car starts to swerve in another lane. "Baby I'm sorry." She says, pulling his dick out his pants and

sucking it.

Jahmere manages to find a parking spot. "Shiit" he says. Pushing her head down on his dick. "Show me

how sorry you really are" he says face fucking her mouth. Namira can feel herself gagging, but she

doesn't stop sucking. She picks up the speed, sucking his dick even faster. "Aww fuck!" Jahmere says

cumin in Namira's mouth. She smiles, swallowing every last drop. "Do you accept my apology" giving

him the sad eyes.

"I'm think about, it while you go and back us an overnight bag." Jahmere says pulling into the parking

garage. "For what" Namira asks.

"See this is why we always fucking beefin." Jahmere says turning the car off. "You ask too many

fucking questions."

"Okay, baby I'm sorry." Namira says. 'You right." She says, getting out the car and going up to their

condo to pack a bag.

Jahmere decides to check his messages. While he waits for Namira, to get back down to the car.

"Good Afternoon Mr. Lawson this is Dr. Mandolin from Lankenau Hospital regarding a Va'Shay

Lawson." "You were listed as her emergency contact and if you be so kind to call the hospital at-"

Namira comes back to the car. Jahmere ends the voicemail, and puts his phone on the charger. She has

the Lou duffle and her suitcase. Namira puts it in the back seat of the car. "Baby I'm ready." She says

getting back in, the passenger side of the car. Jahmere looks in the backseat. "Aye yo, I said a duffle

bag."

"What I need options." Namira say. "So, where we going to anyway. Jahmere shakes his head and

starts the car. "The Ritz Carlton downtown."

"Opp zaddy you fancy huh." Namira says kissing him on his lips. Sitting back in the seats and enjoying

the ride.

"I just wanted to do something, so we could relax." Jahmere says, caressing Namira's thigh. "Shit been

crazy between the two of us."

"Yea, it has." Namira says. She doesn't want to ruin the moment, but him telling her about his mother.

It starting to get to her. *"Does he think I'm crazy?" "Like I'm not able to take care of myself.* She says

to herself, but is interrupted. Jahmere gets out the car, as they pull up to the Ritz Carlton. He opens the

passenger side door. So Namira can get out, and gets the suitcase and duffle bag out the backseat. He

hands his keys to the Valet, and they head inside of the hotel.

Jahmere, and Namira arrive at the Ritz Carlton. They walk towards the front desk to check in.

"Good evening." The hotel attendant says.

"I have a reservation for Jahmere." "Last name Lawson." Jahmere says, to the front desk attendant.

"Okay, give me a moment." The attendant says, typing the name in the computer. "It looks like,

somebody is already checked in, by that name."

"What you mean?" Jahmere says, with confusion on his face.

"Yes, a Quinel Lawson." The attendant replies.

"Ohh naw." Jahmere says, letting out a sigh of relief. He pulls out his id, and says. "My name is

Jahmere Lawson." "My apologies." The attendant says, correcting the issue.

Namira walks up to Jahmere, and says. "Baby, everything okay." She says, kissing him on her cheek.

"How many keys will you need?" The attendant asks, Jahmere. "Two please." Namira says instantly.

"Okay, there you go." The attendant says, handing the keys to Namira. "Enjoy your stay, at the Ritz

Carlton."

They get on the elevator, and head up to the second floor. They get off, and walk to their hotel room.

Room 240, and go inside. "This room is gorgeous baby." Namira says. Noticing the champagne,

sitting in the ice bucket.

"Yea it is." Jahmere says, admiring the room. "I'm hit the shower, and get dressed."

"Okay baby." Namira says sitting on the couch. She grabs a champagne glass, and pours herself a

glass. She walks over to the couch, and she sits her purse on the seat of the couch. She pulls out her

phone, checking to see if she has any missed calls.

Particularly, from Leelee. She wanted to go over the plan, to get rid of Va'Shay permanently. Leelee

doesn't answer, so Namira leaves her a message. *"When you get this, call me."*

"Ard, bye hoe." She says, before she hangs up. Namira takes her charger out her suitcase. She plugs

up her phone, and strips naked. So, she can join Jahmere in the shower.

About an hour later. They are both dressed, and ready to go. Jahmere is wearing some, Armani

exchange boot cut jeans. A Lacoste button up shirt, a gold Rolex watch, and a brand-new pair of

Balmain sneaks. Namira wore a Christian Dior, halter strap dress. Some Louis Vuitton heels, with the

matching bag. She complements the look, with some gold hoop earrings. Namira adds her YSL

lipstick, in red to her lips. "Damn baby you look good." Jahmere says, admiring her outfit.

"So, do you zaddy." Namira says, spraying her Osca De' Larenta perfume. "Where are we going

anyway?"

"It's a surprise." Jahmere says, not wanting to ruin the surprise. "Don't worry bae." He says opening

the door. "Ya man gotchu." He says, as they are heading to the elevator. Jahmere checks his pants and

notices he doesn't have his wallet. "Aww shit."

"What's wrong baby?" Namira asks, noticing the irritation on his face.

"I gotta get my wallet." Jahmere says. "Go ahead down, cause the town car waiting." He says, as he is

walking back to their room.

"Okay baby." Namira says, walking towards the elevator. As she is walking, she hears a *"stop."* She

stops dead in her tracks. Namira turns around and sees Leelee, they both freezes.

"Ohh hey girl." Leelee says chuckling, nervously. "Bih, what you doing here?"

"I called ya ass." Namira says. Noticing Leelee's uncomfortableness.

"Ohh forreal." Leelee says, playing it off. "My phone must have been turned off."

"Mmhmm." Namira says, folding her arms. "I guess you, and Bah back together then, huh." She says,

referring to the fact. She is dressed in a robe.

"Umm naw, see." Leelee begins to say, but Jahmere walks up interrupting them.

"Aye yo sis, wassup?!" Jahmere says, surprised to see Leelee. "What you doing here?" He asks, giving

her a hug.

"Ohh nothing, just getting a little break." Leelee begins to say. Quinel opens the hotel room door, and

says. "Aye babe- "He stops, when he sees Jahmere, and Namira standing there. "Shit" he says.

"Quin?!" Namira says. "What the fuck is going on!"

"See." Quinel says, wrapping his arms around Leelee's waist, and smiling.

"Everybody get the fuck in the room." Jahmere says. "Now!" Pushing Leelee and Quinel in the room.

"So, you fucking married men now." Namira says with an attitude. Snapping on Leelee.

"Mira, a-" Leelee begins to speak, but Namira puts her hand up. "Save it bitch." Namira says. She

turns to Jahmere. "Baby lets go."

"Naw." Jahmere says, walking up to his brother. "I want to know, what the fuck is going on."

"My nigga, chill." Quinel says, noticing how pissed he is. "I was going to tell you."

"So, this why you wanted to move back to Philly?" Jahmere says, in a pissed off tone.

"Yea." Quinel says with hesitancy. "And no." He says chuckling.

"Lee, let me speak to you." Namira says. Dragging her, into the next room.

"Ohh sis." Leelee says, trying to change the conversation. Them shoes, is poppin on you."

"Cut the bullshit." Namira says. "What the fuck, is going on here?" She demands. "Does he even know?" Namira asks, folding her arms. Waiting for Leelee to answer her question.

"Know what." Leelee says, rolling her eyes with irritation.

"Lee, don't play dumb." Namira says. "Does he know, you pregnant!" She says loudly.

"Sssh!" Leelee says. "Lower ya fucking tone." She says, not wanting Quinel to hear.

"No bitch!" Namira demands. "What the fuck is you doing?" She asks, crossing her arms.

"To answer your question." Leelee says, letting out a sigh. "No, he doesn't." She rolls her eyes, sitting on the bed. "Tuesday, I'm getting rid of the baby." Leelee says with an attitude. "So, that solves that."

Namira just shakes her head. "Lee you not right." Walking over to the bed, sitting next to her. "How long, have ya'll two been creeping?"

"Umm, remember when we were in New York?" Leelee says confessing.

"Omg, bitch that long!" Namira says, raising her voice. "Wasn't you, and Bah was still together." She asks, with confusion.

"Mira listen." Leelee says. "I know it looks bad." She says to Namira. "On some real shit, I Love him." Leelee says, lowing her tone. Namira just give Leelee this look, as if to say *"bitch, this is bad."*

Namira takes a deep breath, before speaking. "What, ya'll together or something?"

"I'm not sure." Leelee says. "It's complicated." She says, shrugging her shoulders.

Namira just rolls her eyes. "Lee, this ain't cool." She is starting to get pissed off. Namira thought, she wouldn't have to deal with anymore drama.

"I know that Mira." Leelee says, with irritation in her voice. "Him, and Jaz not even the fuck married."

"Yea, sure." Namira says, with a scoff. Leelee goes into the living room. Grabbing Quinel's divorce papers, off the table. Marching back into the room, handing them to Namira. "Read them."

"It still doesn't make it right." Namira says taking the papers, reading the document. Sure enough, Leelee is right. *"I'm surprised Jazmine, didn't mention this to me, over the phone."* She says to herself.

Chapter 15

Back in the Living Room

"The fuck is going on?" Jahmere asks, waiting for Quinel to answer. Trying to figure out why, he didn't mention him and Leelee.

 "I know it looks bad." Quinel says, chuckling, not seeing what the big deal is.

"Nigga, this shit not funny." Jahmere says. "Is you stupid, she is married." Jahmere says, referring to Bahshere.

"Fuck that snake ass nigga!" Quinel says, with hatred in his voice. "He ain't loyal-" He begins to say, but Namira and Leelee. Come walking into the living room "Baby, let's go." Namira says, grabbing Jahmere's arm.

"We going finish, this convo bro." Jahmere says to Quinel. "Real shit." He says, as they leave.

Leelee walks up to Quinel, and says. "I feel so bad." She lays her head on his chest. "I don't want it to be beef, between ya'll." Leelee says, letting out a sigh.

"Let me handle my bro." Quinel says, smacking Leelee on her ass. "Its all good." He walks over to her, kissing on her lips. Laying her back into the bed. "I told you I got this." Quinel says, tracing the outline of her lips, and looking her in her eyes. "You trust me right.

Back at Lankenau Hospital

Slowly, Va'Shay opens her eyes. "Where am I?" She asks, in a panicking tone. Things are a little fuzzy. All Va'Shay remembers, is hearing Bahshere voice. Speaking of Bahshere, he comes walking in the room. Looking good as ever, with his trimmed goatee, and thin mustache. Fresh haircut, denim jeans, and new Jordan's. "Hey zaddy." Va'Shay says with a smile. As he hands the bouquet of roses to her. She hands them to the nurse, and says to her. "Can you find me something, to put these in?" She says to the nurse says, as she is leaving the room.

"You finally woke up huh." Bahshere says, grabbing a chair. Pulling it up, sitting by the side of the bed.

"Yea, I'm okay." Va'Shay manages to say. Sitting up in the bed, so she can make herself comfortable.

"We got a problem-" Bahshere begins to say, but the doctor comes in. "Mr. Lawson you got my message." He doctor says with excitement.

"Who are you?" Va'Shay asks, trying to figure out what is going on.

"My apologies." He says with a chuckle. "Dr Mandolin had to do ER surgery." "My name is Dr Izaba." He says, pulling out Va'Shay chart, and going over the doctors notes.

"So how is she doing doc?" Bahshere asks, trying to get to what is important. Va'Shay's health.

"Much better, according to her tests." Dr Izaba says. "The swelling has gone down completely." He says with a smile. "She will be released in a few days."

"You think, you can back a little later." Va'Shay says. "I want to talk to my husband in private." She says, smiling at Bahshere. "If you don't mind."

"Sure, no problem." Dr Izaba says, before leaving the room. Va'Shay starts laughing, at the last comment that she made.

Bahshere looks at Va'Shay and says. "I ain't ya husband." He says with an attitude. "Leelee knows about us."

"What, how?!" Va'Shay says, getting upset.

"I think it was Namira." Bahshere says. "It's only a matter of time, before Jah finds out."

"Man, fuck that nigga, and that bitch!" Va'Shay says, getting hype.

"Chill yo." Bahshere says, sucking his teeth.

"That's easy for you to say." Va'Shay says snapping. "Wait, till I run into them. She says slyly. "You keep playing on his good side." Va'Shay says, caressing Bahshere face.

"This why I fuck with you." Bahshere says, pulling Va'Shay closer to him.

"Ohh you already know" Va'Shay says smiling, looking into Bahshere eyes.

The nurse comes back, with the vase of roses. "Where would you like these?" She asks, Va'Shay.

"Over there." Va'Shay says, pointing to the window. The nurse leaves back out the room. "Now, where was we." She says turning her attention. Back to Bahshere, kissing him on his lips.

Kimmel Center(Center City)

"Can you believe her." Namira says with a scoff, looking out the window. Trying to figure out where are they going.

"Namira just chill out." Jahmere says, kissing her on the lips. "Listen, her and my brother go way back."

"So." Namira says, turning to face Jahmere. "He married." "I mean *was* married to Jaz."

"So what." Jahmere says, getting a little annoyed. "They not together anymore." He says, pointing out the obvious.

"Okay baby, you right I'm sorry." Namira says, sitting back and enjoying the ride.

The town car pulls up, to the Kimmel Center. Namira has been hinting to Jahmere. That she wanted to see the hip-hop opera. He thought this would be, the perfect surprise for her. Just the two of them, with no distractions. It's been rough, the last few weeks. He helps Namira out of the car. "Aww baby, you remembered." Namira says in excitement. "Yea, you were bugging me for weeks." Jahmere says chuckling. They head into the opera to enjoy their night......

Back at the Ritz Carlton

Quinel is laying in the bed with Leelee, smoking the rest of the dutch. It's a lot of things on his mind. The one thing, that is really eating him up, is Bahshere. That night of the set up, Quinel was on his way over to Say'Von crib. So he could squash the beef, between him and Jahmere. When Quinel pulled up, he heard gunshots. Just when, he was about to get out of his car. He saw Va'Shay darting right past him. She was running so fast, that she didn't even notice Quinel.

So, Quinel followed her, which led him to Va'Shay, getting out of Say'Von Lexus. She walks over, and gives Bahshere a sensual hug. Quinel couldn't make out, what Bahshere was saying to Va'Shay. Quinel just saw Va'Shay, give the duffle of money, to Bahshere. It didn't take Quinel, long to put it all together. His gut already confirmed, what he already knew. The vibration of his phone, interrupts his thoughts. Quinel looks at the caller id. He really doesn't want, to answer the phone. "Yo." Quinel says in a hushed tone. He looks over at Leelee, who is sound asleep. Careful not to wake Leelee up, he gets out the bed, and walks into the living room area. "What do you want?" Quinel asks. Not wanting to deal, with Jazmine and her bullshit.

"I'm sorry baby." Jazmines says, crying on the phone. "Please, take me back." She says begging.

"Naw ma, I'm good." Quinel says, as he hangs up the phone. Honestly, he doesn't even feel bad for Jazmine.

He knew better, but being the type of nigga that he is. Quinel tried to look past her ways, but eventually they came to the light. He goes back to the bedroom, and finds Leelee sitting up in the bed, titties out. "Zaddy, you good?" Leelee asks, sealing up the dutch.

"Yea, ma I'm straight." Quinel says, sitting his phone on the table.

"You sure?" Leelee asks again. Looking at him, but not distracting her from sparking up.

"Yea." Quinel says, getting back in bed with her. "This shit, is about to get mad crazy."

"Yea, I know." Leelee says, taking a long drag. Letting the weed smoke, fill the air. She hands the dutch to Quinel. He takes a pull on it, before saying. "How about you, come stay with a nigga in New York, for a lil bit?" Passing the dutch back to her. "You can do all the shopping you want, in Manhattan."

"That does sound like a good idea." Leelee says. "I can't right now." She says, letting out a sigh. She has to get the abortion done. Plus, she doesn't even want Quinel to even know. It wouldn't just be right, with all the bullshit that is going on.

"Why ma?" Quinel asks, kissing her on her neck.

"Me and Namira, got a situation we gotta handle." Leelee says, taking the L from Quinel.

"Oh word, say no more." Quinel says, not pressing the issue any further.

"Once, I handle this." Leelee says, climbing on top of Quinel. "Then, I'm all yours." She says, kissing his lips. He puts the L out in the astray, and caresses Leelee body. "I Love you yo." He says, gently grabbing on her face.

Hip-Hop Opera (Center City)

Namira and Jahmere, are enjoying the opera. Jahmere phone begins to ring. He looks down at the caller id, he doesn't recognize the number. So, he lets it go to voicemail. It begins to ring again, this time he excuses himself.

"Where are you going?" Namira asks, as Jahmere leaves out the opera.

Jahmere walks in the hallway, of the opera. He answers the call, and says "Who dis?"

"Hello, is this Mr. Lawson?" The voice, on the other end of the call asks.

"Yea, who dis?" Jahmere asks again, not recognizing the voice.

"This is the doctor Mandolin." Dr Mandolin says with hesitancy. "I had left you a message."

"Yea my bad doc." Jahmere says, letting out a sigh of relief.

"It's fine." Dr Mandolin says. "We do have a issue, that needs to be handled." He says with concerned tone.

"Okay, I'll be right there." Jahmere says, as he hangs up. He heads back into the opera.

"Is everything okay baby?" Namira asks with worry, but trying to enjoy the opera.

"Yea." Jahmere says, trying to get his thoughts together. "I gotta handle something." He says, kissing Namira on her cheek. "You stay right here, and enjoy yourself."

"The fuck Jah, like you gotta be playing." Namira says with a scoff. Not believing the bullshit.

"I'm meet you for dinner." Jahmere says, as he leaves out the opera. He leaves out the Kimmel Center, and flags down a cab. He tells the cab driver, to take him to Lankenau hospital. Jahmere can't help, but feel sorry for Va'Shay. Even though their marriage is over. He still can't total dismiss her totally. Jahmere is really worried, for sake of the kids. Despite the fact, the kids aren't his.

Twenty minutes later, the cab pulls up to the emergency department of Lankenau. Jahmere pays the cab driver, and gets out. Making his way, into the emergency room, and walking up the receptionist. "Damn, you fine as shiit." The receptionist says. Looking Jahmere up, and down. He ignores her comment, and says: "I'm here to see a Va'Shay Lawson."

"Yes, have a seat with ya fine ass." The receptionist says. "I'm page the doctor." He has a seat, waiting for the doctor to come out. Maybe, fifteen minutes later, Dr Mandolin comes out. "Hey Mr. Lawson."

"Wassup doc, everything good?" Jahmere asks in a rushed tone.

"I just wanted to touch bases with you." Dr Mandolin says, looking over Va'Shay chart. "That's strange." He says, going through the paperwork. "It seems, you already signed the release forms."

"What forms?" Jahmere asks, not knowing what the doctor is talking about.

"The forms about Mrs. Lawson, being released." Dr Mandolin explains. "It seems that last name is different."

"Who signed them?" Jahmere asks, feeling a headache beginning to form.

"It appears a Bahshere." "His last name is Peterson?" Dr Mandolin says, showing the signature to Jahmere.

"The fuck is he doing?" Jahmere says to himself. Not wanting to get upset, or jump to any

conclusions.

"It seems that earlier today." Dr Mandolin, begins to explain. "I was in the operating room and another

doctor took over for me." He says looking at the notes. That was written in Va'Shay's chart. "Let me

go talk to the nurse, and get this figured out." Dr Mandolin says, with confusion. "In the meantime,

would you like to go back?" He says, closing Va'Shay's chart.

"Yea sure." Jahmere says wanting to make sure, Va'Shay is good. Dr Mandolin escorts, Jahmere to her

room. He stops and says to Jahmere. "Let me get a new set of forms." "You can go right on in."

"Okay, cool." Jahmere says, as he walks toward Va'Shay's room.

As he is walking, into the room. Jahmere sees Va'Shay, and Bahshere kissing. "The fuck is going on!"

He says, not believing what the fuck he is seeing. Bahshere's facial expression looks as if. He has seen

a ghost. Bahshere gets off the bed, and walks towards Jahmere. "We need to talk."

Va'Shay interrupts and says. "Naw, fuck him Bah." She says, rolling her eyes. "We *been* fucking,

behind ya back." Va'Shay says with no remorse. Not caring how it sounded.

"Shut the fuck up, Shay." Bahshere says, cutting his eyes at her. He doesn't know what to say. Jahmere

is really trying, not to lose his cool. He really wants to pop, both of them. Then again, he knows it's not

going to end well, for his sake. "You supposed to be my right hands." Jahmere says, walking up to

Bahshere. His trigger finger is itching, but he gotta keep his cool.

"Yo bro." Bahshere says. "I-I'm sorry, shit just-" He stammers, trying to find the right words.

"Fuck it." Jahmere says, throwing his hands up. "She was just a hoe, anyway." He says smiling, putting his hand on Bahshere shoulder.

"Fuck you Jah!" Va'Shay yells, from the hospital bed. Something about Jahmere's coolness, sent a chill down, Bahshere's spine.

Jahmere walks out the hospital room, the doctor is calling his name, but he ignores him. Walking, directly out the hospital. Vowing to get revenge, on Bahshere and Va'Shay. Jahmere phone starts to ring, again. He answers with a "yo."

"Ain't no fucking yo!" Namira says. "What the fuck was that earlier?!" She yells at him, through the phone.

"Baby, I'm on my way." Jahmere says trying to hide his anger. Not wanting to ruin their evening.

"Yea, whatever." Namira says, with an attitude, hanging up. Jahmere gets in the cab. He rests his head, against the back seat. His mind is racing, all he is feeling right now. Is rage. He would have never thought, Bahshere would cross him.

The word in the Philly streets, was that Bahshere and Va'Shay. They are the ones, who set up Say'Von. Now, that Jahmere thinks about it, it's all make sense. Bahshere wanting to be there Even, knowing Namira's movements, all because of Bahshere dumbass. Jahmere slams his fist, into the back of the cab headrest. The cab driver stops. "Sir, are you okay?" He asks, looking at Jahmere through the rearview mirror. "Yea, just keep driving." Jahmere says, rubbing his hand. He just lets his mind wonder, as the cab drives through the city traffic.

The driver pulls up to the Maggiano's on Filbert street. Jahmere pays the cab driver, and gets out. He fixes his clothes, and takes a deep breath. Jahmere is trying to keep his cool, and not let what just happened effect him. Jahmere heads into the Maggiano's. "Good Evening sir" the host says, greeting Jahmere with a smile.

"I have a reservation, under Lawson." Jahmere says, not showing irritation in his voice.

"Ah yes." The host says, grabbing a menu. "The other party has already arrived, and been seated." He says, leading Jahmere is over to the table. "Follow me, right this way."

"Finally, you get here." Namira says, with sarcasm. Looking up from her menu, and rolling her eyes.

"My bad baby." Jahmere says, kissing Namira on the lips. "Had to handle some fucking shit." He says, taking a seat. Pouring him a glass of champagne.

The waitress comes up, and asks. "Are you guys ready to order?" She says, in a cheerful voice.

"Yes." Namira says, as she looks over the menu.

Jahmere order his food first. "Can I have the center cut, Filet Mignon."

"Sure." the waitress says, writing down his order. "How would you like your steak?"

"Well done, no pink in the middle." Jahmere says, trying to relax. "Also, could I have shot of cognac."

"Do you have a preference?" The waitress asks Jahmere.

"Don't matter." Jahmere says. He really is trying, to take the edge off.

"And what about you?" The waitress asks, turning to Namira.

"I'm have the Shrimp Fra Diavolo." Namira says, scanning the menu again. Deciding if, she wanted something else to order.

"Would you like, something to drink?" The waitress asks Namira.

"Can you bring me, a glass of Chardonnay." Namira says, handing her menu to the waiter.

"Okay." She says collecting the menus. "I will put your orders in, and be back with your drinks" she says, walking away.

"You know, you missed a good opera." Namira says to Jahmere. As she unfolds her napkin, placing it on her lap.

"Aww, babe I'm sorry." Jahmere says, not trying to be pissed.

"Mmhmm." Namira says, eyeing Jahmere suspiciously. Noticing how his attitude has changed, ever since he got to dinner.

The waitress comes back, with their drinks. Jahmere takes the shot of cognac straight back. "Can I get another." He says, handing the glass to the waitress. "Can you make it, a double."

"Sure." The waitress says. Taking the glass, and leaving the table again.

The food arrives shortly, and they are enjoying their food. Jahmere phone begins to ring. He looks at the caller id, and it's the hospital. Jahmere sucks his teeth, as he forwards the call to voicemail.

"Everything good?" Namira asks, putting a piece of shrimp. In her mouth, and taking a sip of Chardonnay.

"Yea, babe, how is your food." Jahmere asks, trying to change the subject.

"Great." Namira says, with a quickness. "Who is that, calling ya phone?" Namira asks, with an attitude.

"Can we enjoy, the rest of tonight." Jahmere says, with a sigh. Namira just rolls her eyes. She knows when something is wrong. *"First he leaves the opera."* Namira says, to herself. *"I know he hiding something."* Namira is holding the glass of wine, in her hand. Eyeing Jahmere, before she takes another sip.

Jahmere waves the waitress over, so she can bring the check. He is ready for them to leave. Jahmere wants to spend, the rest of the night. Relaxing with Namira, he doesn't need any *"I told you so"* from Namira. He decides not telling her, is the best option. The waiter comes back with the check. Interrupting Jahmere's thoughts, he pays for the food and leaves a nice tip. Him and Namira leave out the restaurant. The cool air hit their faces, as they wait for the town car to pull up.

"So, you still not going to tell me." Namira says. "You right." She says, still trying to press the issue. Jahmere lets out this big sigh. "You really starting to get, on my fucking nerves."

"Who the fuck!" Namira says, raising her voice. "Is you getting smart with nigga!" She yells crossing her arms. The town car pulls up, and Jahmere helps Namira in. He gets into the car, and looks out the window. Jahmere is not paying, any attention to Namira. As the town car, drives through the city. His mind is too occupied, by what he seen at the hospital. Just him thinking about it, is making his blood boil.

The car pulls up, to the entrance of the Ritz Carlton. Namira is the first to get out. "I'm find out what's up." She says, grabbing her purse and slamming the door.

Jahmere takes his time getting out. He really can't deal with Namira, and her attitude right now. If anybody should be mad and upset, it should be him. He walks into the lobby, and sends Quinel a text: *"Be at ya room in like 10 minutes, it's a situation."*

Jahmere phone starts to ring again. It's the hospital, he answers. "Mr. Lawson." Dr Mandolin says, with hesitancy. "You left the hospital, without signing the paperwork." He says.

"Yea, listen doc." Jahmere says, trying his best to keep his cool. "The bul that is in there with Va'Shay Thompson." He says. "He will be acting, as her emergency contact."

"I'm not understanding." Dr Mandolin says, with a bit of confusion.

"Me and her are no longer together." Jahmere says. "The bul in the room, with Va'Shay." "Is who, you want to talk to." Jahmere hangs up, catching the elevator up to their room. He uses the key card, to go into their hotel room. "Mira!" he yells, through the hotel room. "Mira!" He yells, tossing the key card, on the table. Jahmere heads toward their bedroom, he finds Namira taking off her dress, and earrings.

"Baby, listen." Jahmere says, walking towards Namira. "I promise you, there is nothing wrong." He says. Trying his best, to hide his frustration.

"There you go!" Namira says, getting pissed off. "Fucking lying to me, again Jah!" She says, cutting her eyes at him. "I know, when ya dumb ass is lying." She says to Jahmere. "What, you don't trust me."

"Aye yo." Jahmere says. "You know, I trust you with my life." Jahmere says, caressing her cheek.

"What are you not, telling me!" Namira demands, really wanting to know. She feel that something is wrong.

Jahmere just snaps, and says. "Cause its none of ya motherfucking concern!"

"Who the fuck!" "You yelling at!" Namira yells, getting in Jahmere face.

"Man take ya ass to sleep." Jahmere says getting an attitude. "I be back" he says, walking out the bedroom.

Namira is right on Jahmere heels. She refuses, to just let it go. "Where are you going Jah?" She yells back at him. Jahmere continues to ignore Namira. He leaves out their hotel room. So, he can talk to Quinel. The way he is feeling right now, he wants kill Va'Shay and Bahshere.

To Be Continued